Taking the Reins

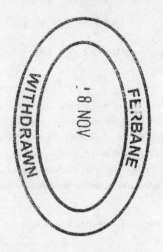

Published in the UK by Scholastic Children's Books, 2020
Euston House, 24 Eversholt Street, London, NW1 1DB
A division of Scholastic Limited

London – New York – Toronto – Sydney – Auckland
Mexico City – New Delhi – Hong Kong

First published in the US by Alfred A. Knopf, an imprint of Random House
Children's Books, a division of Penguin Random House LLC, New York.

Text © Jane Smiley, 2020

The right of Jane Smiley to be identified as the author of this work has been
asserted by her under the Copyright, Designs and Patents Act 1988.

ISBN 978 1407 18444 9

Printed by CPI Group (UK) Ltd, Croydon, CR0 4YY
Papers used by Scholastic Children's Books are made from wood grown in
sustainable forests.

1 3 5 7 9 10 8 6 4 2

www.scholastic.co.uk

Taking the Reins

JANE SMILEY

SCHOLASTIC

Taking the Reins

CHAPTER 1

You could say it was my birthday present. First, Mom said that I could go to the big show for both weeks. This didn't mean Monday through Friday, like school, but a class on Thursday, a class on Friday, two classes on Saturday, and then watching Abby take Gee Whiz over some big jumps and out onto the outside course on Sunday, then the same the second week. After that, it was like Abby was polishing me and polishing Tater, my pony, and making sure that we were clean as a whistle inside and out. Mom even sent the black show jacket that Jane gave us (used but in good condition) to the cleaners. Now it was the second week. The first week had gone pretty well – Tater and I got a third, a fourth, and a fifth. Did he have fun? No one will ever know.

Tater and I had been practising since Christmas, when Mom and Dad gave him to me, the best Christmas present ever – that was six and a half months ago. Since we now live fifteen minutes from Abby's place, I get to go there three days a week. Mom and Dad pay for two lessons, and I pay for a third one by mucking stalls, cleaning tack, sweeping the barn aisle and the tack room, and, yes, standing around and staring at Ned in the ring, out in the pasture, in a stall every once in a while. He is, as Abby's dad said, "coming along," but he's still mysterious and hard to handle. If I said that he's not mysterious to me, Abby's dad would think I am out of my mind, so I don't say anything, but I keep my eyes open. Tater is much more grown-up than Ned – he has already "come along," and riding him is always safe (Mom would say, "Thank goodness for that!") and always fun. It's safe because even if I fell off (which I did once), it isn't very far to the ground, and it's fun because I learn something new in every lesson.

Dad likes making the trip back and forth to pick me up, because one of his jobs at the Ford dealer is driving cars around – especially the trade-ins, to see how they run and what repairs they might need. (When someone wants to buy a new car, they give the dealer the old car and get some money for it, which the dealer subtracts from the price of the new car.) It's fun – I never know whether he's going to show up in a Fairlane or a Mustang or an old Chevy. Once, in the spring, he showed up in a car just like the first car he ever owned, a green Studebaker from 1950. He and Abby's dad stood around and talked about the car for ten minutes, and then looked under the hood. It wasn't like any car you see today, long and straight and sort of flat. The Studebaker had little round headlights like eyeballs. In fact, it was rounded all over, as if it were made of clay.

Abby's dad drove us to the show, which is at the stables where I first learned to ride, where Jane teaches riding, and is about half an hour from Abby's ranch. I sat in the middle. Abby sat by the window. I listened to her and her dad talking about every little thing, and I thought it was exhausting. But when we got there, and Rodney came out to greet us (and handed me a scone that he had made) and Jane gave me a hug, and then Blue saw us from the first stall in the barn and whinnied loud and clear, all the tired part went away. And I realized that here I was, eleven years old, and whatever might happen, I was going to have the time of my life.

I went to Tater's stall and gave him a carrot. He didn't nicker, but he did come over and take the carrot nicely, and everything was fine until I looked up, and there was a kid by the roof sitting on one of those beams that goes from one side of the barn to the other. He was looking down at me, and when I saw him, he burst out laughing. I shied, but Tater didn't. I pretended not to be looking at the kid, but I was. Soon he was tiptoeing along the beam like a tightrope walker in a circus. I walked out of the barn; Jane was explaining something to Abby, who was standing there with Gee Whiz, and I said, "Do you know there's an intruder?"

"An intruder?" Jane looked out toward the arena.

"In the barn."

"Oh, that's Da. He's not—" Then her eyes opened wide, and she said, "What is he doing now?"

I said, "He's up by the roof, walking along the beam."

Jane ran into the barn and I followed her, but by that time, this kid, "Da," was sitting on the bench by the tack room, pulling on his boot. Sunshine was coming in the windows, and I could see him better. He was small, maybe smaller than I am. He had long legs and big hands, and was a little strange-looking, and I knew right then and there that he was one of those bad boys like Jimmy Murphy. (Jimmy isn't a bad boy anymore, or at least is trying very hard not to be, since he won the county spelling contest at the end of the school year by spelling "efficacious" and he also said what it meant, which you have to do in our spelling contest.) But unlike every bad boy I've ever known, as soon as he got his boot on, Da jumped up, gave me a big smile, and said, "You're Ellen! Jane said you were coming. She said that you're almost as hard to put up with as I am!" Then all three of us laughed.

And maybe it wasn't very nice of me to say, "Da? Why would you be named Da? It sounds like 'Duh.'"

Jane gave me a look, but Da said, "It's really David, but I like Da better."

And, to be honest, I like people who know their own minds, so that was enough for me.

Then the business of the day began. At first, there was fog everywhere, grey and dense, hiding the trees and settling over the jumping arena like smoke, but a few dots of blue appeared up above, and the fog began to flutter and rise and float away. I went to Tater's stall, put his halter on, and led him to the cross-ties. I started grooming him with the soft brush – we'd given him a bath the day before, and he'd worn a blanket overnight, so what I had to do was smooth him all over. One reason I like brushing him is that he's a red roan. His head is red-gold, his mane is mostly brown, with some white hairs, and his body is mostly white, but sprinkled with red. He likes being brushed, which is a good thing, since when he's dirty, you can see it a mile away, as my grandma would say. I was thinking all of these things when Rodney came and asked me if I needed any help, and without a second thought, I said, "No thanks."

A lot has changed in the last year. When I started coming to the barn and riding Melinda's pony, I was only seven, and for three years, I thought that Rodney was supposed to do everything – clean the horse, carry the saddle, hoist me up, lead me to the arena. Now I am so used to doing it all myself that it was easier to keep at it. (Abby can't do everything, and she has plenty to do, since at their ranch, they don't hire anyone and do all the work, and they have twelve horses.) Rodney brought me the saddle and pad, gave me a wink, said, "Now ye'll be doin' me out of a job, miss." But we both know that isn't true.

I took the saddle and pad and lifted them onto Tater, up by the withers, then eased them backward, till they settled in against his spine. I went around behind Tater, staying close to his haunches, petting him a little though he never kicks. Then I checked that everything on the right side was even and smooth, let down the girth, and went back to the left side, reached under Tater's chest for the girth, and buckled it tightly enough to hold the saddle in place. Tater pinned his ears for a moment, but some horses kick when you buckle the girth, and Abby says, yes, it is uncomfortable; would you want a strap around your chest? Then I undid the cross-ties and put on Tater's bridle, which has a French link snaffle bit (I love those words); buckled the noseband and the throatlatch; and led Tater out to the mounting block, where I tightened the girth, climbed the two steps, and got on. The whole time, Rodney was shaking his head in his funny way, as if he disapproved, but really meaning that he was happy that I was growing up. Everyone is happy that I'm growing up, including me.

Our class was a pony hunter class. Da was already in the practice arena, also on a pony. There are three sizes of ponies – small, medium, and large. Tater is a medium, which means that he is more than 12.2 hands but less than 13.2. Tater is 13.1 hands plus a half inch. If he stood on his tiptoes, he might be a large pony. A hand is four inches, so at the top of his withers, he is 4'5½". (I always wonder, why don't they train them to rear up and measure them from the tops of their heads, the way they do people?) I am 15 hands to the top of my head, or, as the nurse says when she measures you, 5' tall. At least, I was when I went for a checkup in the spring, but my show pants do seem a little shorter now than they did in March.

I walked toward the practice ring. Da and his pony were trotting, but then they started rocketing around the ring. The pony was a dark grey with a long tail. I paused at the gate to watch. Da sat up, the pony made a sharp turn, then went down over two jumps, an oxer and a panel. Jane said, "Nicely done, now—"

And just then, Da turned again, this time to the left, and raced toward the coop at the end of the prac- tice arena and jumped over it, onto the outside course. After two seconds, I couldn't see him anymore. Jane shook her head, put her hands on her hips, shook her head again, and here he came, back over the coop, and I know that coop is three feet three inches high. I've looked at it lots of times but never dared to jump it be- cause it seems like if you did, you would be heading out into a big, scary world – jumping out at a *gallop* gives me a little shock every time I think of it. Da stopped in front of Jane and said, "I'm warmed up now," and he walked over to the show arena. This I had to watch. Jane followed him, so obviously she had to watch, too.

He stood by the gate – and why didn't he just jump over it to get in? Pretty soon the gate opened, and the announcer said, "Number nineteen, Little Bighorn, ridden by David Chance." And wasn't that the perfect name for that boy? I wasn't the only one watching – Tater had his ears pricked, and when Da and LB circled at the trot, then moved up into the canter, his gaze followed them. Was Tater memorizing the course? I wouldn't put it past him.

I expected Da and LB to be wild and out of control, but it was like Da turned into a different person. He sat up, slowed down, and paid attention. The course was not very complicated – two jumps along the rail to the right, then one at the far end, then a turn across the middle, over a two-stride in-and-out, then turn to the left and an oxer at the near end, then three nicely spaced panel jumps down the long side. That was eight jumps (an in-and-out counts as one, not two), good for Thursday, which is basically a warm-up day, nothing too difficult. LB looped to the left, came down to the trot, circled, down to the walk, long rein, and then the gate opened and they came out, looking relaxed, sashaying, as if to say, "Top that!" Tater watched them. I was not sure I could top that, but Tater was.

Two rounds later, it was our turn. I'm bigger than Da, and Tater is bigger than LB, and I'm probably older than Da, and Tater is surely older than LB, so we walked into the arena just like we knew what we were doing (and we did win a blue ribbon in March, at a schooling show), but I kept that picture of how David Chance did it in my head, and I watched that picture every step of the way. It was really weird – I could see what he did from afar, and I could see what I was doing up close (my hands on the reins, the bill of my hard hat, the centre of the jumps between Tater's ears, the trees and bits of fog in the distance, the railings of the arena, people looking at us, Jane and Abby standing together, blue sky), and then it was over, and we were walking out through the gate. Tater sighed, which means he is relaxed, and I tried not to smile too much. I tried to look as if the best show ride of my life was no big deal.

And then, ten minutes later, they called six of us into the ring, and I did win, and David Chance was second, and why that was I could not begin to tell you, since he obviously knew much more than I did, but Jane would say that you don't know how the judges will think – you just have to hope for the best.

That was my one class of the day. I walked Tater out, untacked him, put him back in his stall, which I did *not* clean, and left the barn. Da was nowhere to be seen, which was maybe a bad thing, but not my business. Abby and Gee Whiz were in the warm-up. He was white as snow and Abby had on a new jacket, new boots, and new breeches – thanks to Jack So Far, who was in his second year of racing, and had run ten times and won $44,000. (I heard Abby's dad and my dad talking about it when they were looking at the Studebaker.) Most of it went into supporting Jack So Far at the track, and the rest into savings, but Abby did get some boots made specially for her, and the rest of her outfit, too. Someday he would return from the track and end up like Gee Whiz, who raced all over the country, won a lot of money, and retired at nine ready to jump jump jump. He was ready to jump now. Abby had been working with him for a year and a half, and he'd learned to do a thing that racehorses don't have to learn, which was to turn a corner, and then another corner and then another corner – racehorses leap out of the gate and go in a long oval to the finish line, and then they are exhausted so they slow down and walk back to the barn. Since Gee Whiz is very tall and very long from nose to tail, it took him a while to learn to turn, but now he is smooth and flexible like a cat.

They cantered in both directions, then took a few jumps. The warm-up ring was a lot busier now than it had been when Da and I were riding, and horses were going in all directions. Gee Whiz wove himself through them like thread through a needle, and Abby's dad, Mr. Lovitt, was smiling and humming like mad. I ran over to him as Abby came out of the gate and walked along with them as they went to the arena. Gee Whiz was on a long rein, with his head down, but his ears were pricked and his tail was switching, and he knew he was going to have fun.

Abby's course was much higher (three feet nine inches) than mine (two feet six inches), and much more complicated, but all she did was trot a circle, rise into the canter, and watch where she was headed. Gee Whiz did all the rest. Ten jumps. When they came back down to the trot afterward, the people in the stands (there were a few now; there hadn't been any for my class) all clapped, and Gee Whiz sauntered out of the arena like he knew they were clapping for him. I was surprised that he didn't take a bow.

CHAPTER 2

On Friday, Mom dropped me off at the showground around eleven and said that she would be back at two, in time for my class. I know kids who go to summer camp – my old friend Melanie Trevor, still the World's Most Interesting Person, as far as I'm concerned, was probably at summer camp on Mars, since she has been to all the other summer camps in the world. (Yes, I am making this up, but it's fun to think about Melanie hiking around Mars with that look on her face of figuring things out step by step.) For me, this show at the stables is enough summer camp. Mom gave me money for two meals, and I went to the food stand and bought a hot dog with ketchup but *no mustard,* and the woman who was serving me said, "I can hear you; you don't have to shout." Off to my left, I heard a laugh, and after she handed me the hot dog and a lemonade, I turned and saw Da sitting by himself. I looked very closely, but I didn't see anything tying him to his chair, the way you would tie a horse to a hitching post to keep him from running away. I took my food and went and sat at his table. Here is what he had on his plate: a packet of sugar, a carrot, an apple, an oatmeal cookie, a bowl of Cheerios, and a carton of chocolate milk. I said, "Are you a horse? That's horse food."

He laughed again. I decided I liked him, because maybe he was the first person I'd ever met who knew when I was joking, which is pretty much all the time. We started to eat, and I wondered if I'd finally found a friend. Or *the* friend. In my experience, it's very hard to find *the* friend. *The* friend is someone who's always nice to you, who you never see laughing with two other girls after they look at you, who you never hear saying your name in a mean way when you happen to walk into the restroom, someone who does not move her chair apart from you when you sit at her lunch table, someone who, when you make a joke, knows you mean to be funny and laughs. At my old school, my friends were Melanie, who was never mean but didn't know how to laugh, and Jimmy Murphy, who liked to make trouble, run around the block, tell me secrets, and spell long words. At my new school, my friends were Natalie, Jahaira, Maria, and, of all people, Ruthie Creighton, who was my friend from my old school, transformed from a silent girl who always looked down and could not keep her socks pulled up to a happy girl who still didn't say much, who lived in our neighbourhood, and who ran everywhere like she just couldn't contain her joy at having moved out of the fog. But even though my friends came to my birthday party two weeks before the show and brought me some nice presents, I didn't see them much, and summer had been lonely.

Da began to nibble on his carrot as if he were a rabbit, and then he took a big bite of his oatmeal cookie. I said, "What grade are you in?"

"Soon to be fifth."

"I'm going into sixth."

"I would be, but my mom kept me back. My birthday is a day before the cutoff date, and I'm short, so she thought I would get bullied."

"Your mom sounds smart. Where is she?" I looked around.

"She's in Europe for a month. She has a friend, Colonel Dudgeon. They went to look at horses."

"Your mom rides horses?"

"All day, all night. She's the MFH up where we live."

I did not ask him what an MFH was. I thought I would ask Abby.

"That's how she and Aunt Jane got to be friends. They were whippers-in together before Aunt Jane moved down here."

"Our Jane, this Jane, is your aunt?" I felt a little envious.

"Not really, but that's what I'm supposed to call her."

I said, as if I didn't care, "When did you get down here?"

"The day before yesterday."

"It took you a whole day to climb to the roof of the barn?"

He didn't crack a smile. He said, "It was dark when I got here. I did my best."

"Do tell."

"I went out the window of my bedroom, stood on the roof of the garage, and had a good look at the stars over the ocean."

I put my napkin over my mouth, but he could tell I was smiling.

He went on in a deep voice, "For heaven's sake, don't encourage the boy!"

"Who's that?"

Again in a deep voice (he was good at that; it was so deep it almost made my ears tremble), he said, "Colonel Dudgeon, in a high dudgeon."

Now I did laugh. I said, "My grandma uses that expression."

"He's not always in one, but he can get there. My mom says he knows more about horses than anyone else she's ever met."

"I guess he needs to meet Abby's dad. I guess they would have a talk."

"Is he the one with the eyebrows?"

"You noticed."

"I always do."

So, we had a month. I was sure it would be fun.

Mom showed up about halfway through Da's class on Frankenstein, just in time to watch their round. Frankenstein is so lazy that Da had to carry a whip, but he carried it pointing up rather than pointing down, just so Frankie could see it out of the corner of his eye and know it was there. He didn't care. Da did his best, but when Frankie was supposed to canter into the turns and speed up, he would slow down to the trot. Then he would look for the next jump, rise into the canter again, and get over it. He had one rail down.

I then went and did my stuff to get Tater ready for our flat class. For some reason, brushing him made me think of Ned again. I used to talk to Ned when I was younger, before I realized that I was just imagining things. If Abby's dad had got his way, Ned would be here at the show, winning classes and getting ready to be sold for a lot of money. But Ned has been a conundrum (I love that word) because he is good *almost* all the time, but really not good *enough* of the time so that he can be counted on, and when you sell a horse, the new owner wants to count on him (or her). Some horses are handsome and some horses are beautiful. Ned is darling – his coat is so smooth, you want to pet it all the time, and his face is so kind that you just want to hug him. He has very smooth gaits, likes to jump, and so, if only . . . But that "if only" has never happened. So as I was brushing Tater, I worried just a little bit about Ned. I had no idea what Abby's dad would do if he couldn't sell him. Sigh.

However, when I got into the warm-up arena, Da was already there, on a chestnut pony named Pretty Girl, and watching them made me stop thinking about Ned. Pretty Girl was very good-looking, but I saw right off that Da was going to have a hard time with her. Every time a horse got anywhere near her, she put her ears back, and twice she made little squeals. When she squealed, Da tightened his legs so she would trot out a little – that means lengthening her stride, not just going faster – and Jane would say that works because it takes a horse's attention away from whatever is annoying her. Jane also says that mares are more irritable than geldings. Abby says this is because mares are in charge, and the bossy ones need to make sure the others are paying attention and behaving themselves. I can understand this perfectly well because at my school, it looks to me like the girls are in charge, and the popular ones are always making sure that the others are doing what they're supposed to. I do not like doing what I'm supposed to.

I walked Tater over to Da (Pretty Girl gave him a dirty look, but that was all – Tater doesn't offend anyone) and asked, "What happened with Frankie?"

Da said, "Jane stuck me on him. I've never been

on him before, and he was good in the warm-up, so I didn't really know what I was doing."

"You showed a horse that you've never been on before?"

"That's what pros do!" He said this in his Colonel Dudgeon voice and trotted off. Another thing I didn't know.

Now Abby showed up outside the warm-up arena, slid between the rails, and came over. She said, "How's Tater today?"

"Same as yesterday."

"Maybe. See if you can make a little figure eight, trying to stay out of the other horses' way, but also trying to trot evenly and make a good shape."

I trotted about halfway around the arena, almost to the gate, then did my first turn to the right, went around the jumps (it was a hack class, so no one was jumping), turned left. When I came back toward the middle, I realized that I was not actually in the middle, so I didn't think it was very good. Without Abby saying anything, I started over, this time sitting deeper, and with more leg on Tater, who then perked up a little. The way a horse moves comes up through your body, and if it's lively, it makes you see things more sharply and sense things more quickly, as if his eyes and your eyes are now connected. Our second figure eight was much better, and when I stopped to talk to Abby afterward, she said, "Perfect light rein. Your reins are like threads." Once she mentioned it, I remembered it – reins like threads. I said those words in my head, "Reins like threads, reins like threads." Plus, "Sit deep." I was concentrating so much that I didn't notice Da and Pretty Girl or any of the others at all. The announcer called the class and we walked through the gate and across to the main arena, which is huge, and was full of jumps for the next class.

It was a lot more complicated than I thought it would be, because there were twenty of us in there, and I'd never been in a class, or in a lesson, or on a trail ride, where there were twenty ponies and riders. It seemed like the main thing you had to do was not get bumped by someone else or run into a jump. I tried to look ahead, which is what you're supposed to do, and all the time here came someone up on the outside or up on the inside, and if I concentrated too hard, I would be surprised, which is not to say that Tater would be surprised. I could see his ears flicking back and forth and his eyes rolling, and even though his head was straight, he knew they were coming. He wasn't always happy, but he did shift a bit here and a bit there, and we never got bumped, and never ran into a jump. Really, when you see those herds of horses in the movies galloping down hills or across the plains, it's pretty clear that they know a few things that people do not.

I wanted to keep my eye on Da, but I only saw him from time to time. However, every time I saw him, he was over toward the centre of the arena rather than on the rail, which was where I kept Tater. We walked, trotted, turned, trotted, cantered, turned, walked, halted, trotted, and cantered some more, and, eventually, I relaxed, because it took a long time and Tater was watching out for us. His transitions to the canter were really good, and by that I mean that he started to canter when I told him to, but also that he seemed to lift himself up into the canter, and then ease along like a rocking chair. In the second canter, we got near Da, who saw us, and he cocked his head and then nodded, and I knew he meant, "Follow me," and I did. We wove here and there, past the others (and some of the ponies were giving their riders trouble, tossing their heads, refusing to move forward, even breaking to the trot). It seemed like we cantered a long time, and the judge and the woman with him that he was talking to stared at everyone.

Finally the announcer said, "And walk, please!" I sat deep, Da sat deep, and the ponies walked on a loose rein. Tater lowered his head. The announcer called out some numbers for people to stay in the arena – six of them. Da was one and I wasn't, so fourteen of us left. I went to the part of the warm-up area where you could see the arena. It was then that I saw what Da was doing – he was keeping his eye on the judge, and wherever the judge was looking, Da and Pretty Girl were there, following instructions. Two of the other ponies were better-looking and better movers than Pretty Girl. One of them won, and Da came in second. I saw that the key to winning a hack class was being a bit of a pest, meaning that the judge had to see you, and so you had to keep your eye on the judge and make sure that you were where he was looking. Abby had never told me that, but then, Abby doesn't know how to be a pest.

Mom met me by the barn. She said I'd done a good job, and she had a carrot for Tater. I gave her a kiss, and then led Tater into the barn. I felt between his front legs. He was cool, and he kept looking at his stall, so I knew that he wanted to get back to his hay, and who could blame him? I was hungry, too. I wouldn't have thought that a hack class could be so exciting. I did my work. Thank goodness he did not need a bath. All I had to do was brush him where the saddle pad had been and pick his hooves again. It wasn't until I was back out of the barn that I realized that I hadn't given him a kiss or even a pat when I left. But then, he hadn't looked at me, either, because he'd been eating his hay. Yes, I liked Tater, I liked him more and more, but putting him away was like parking your car. All you had to remember was, did you lock the door?

We went to the food tent. Mom ordered me a hot dog without mustard without me even reminding her, and also a chocolate chip cookie. Finally, she said what I knew she was going to say: "You look worn out."

"I am." Then I said, "Where's Joan Ariel?"

"I left her with Grandma. They haven't seen her in two weeks, so they wanted to have her for the day. We're going there for dinner tonight. So what do you want to do for the rest of the afternoon?"

"Take a nap."

"I thought we would stay and watch some other classes."

This should have been exactly what I wanted to do, but I didn't. I was coming back tomorrow. As for today, I'd had enough. And I never thought that I could ever have said that, even to myself.

Mom said, "Let's go to the beach, then. I miss the beach."

I said, "I don't have beach clothes on."

She smiled. "Then let's go buy some. I think you've outgrown everything anyway."

Another thing I never thought could happen – that I could be excited to go to the department store where Mom used to work. So that's what we did. I got two pairs of shorts, a new bathing suit, a pair of sneakers, a package of socks, two blouses, and a pair of sunglasses. And even though Mom doesn't work there anymore, she got her discount. Then we had calamari, and then we walked on the beach, and the waves were tiny and glistening and the sun was brilliant, and we found two whole sand dollars. Which can't be used to buy anything, but look great on the mantel.

Then we went to Grandma and Grandpa's, where

I played with Joan Ariel while Mom and Grandma cooked the spaghetti. Joan Ariel is seventeen months old now, and her favourite thing to do is to jump. She stands in the middle of the room and she waves her arms and then bounces into the air. She doesn't get very far off the ground, and sometimes sits right down without meaning to, but when she does that she just laughs. If I laugh with her, then she jumps even more and laughs even more. I hope that when I was her age, I was as funny as she is, but I doubt it. Dad and Grandpa showed up, and Mom put the spaghetti noodles in the pot of boiling water, and then we spent dinner talking about Dad and Grandpa's golf game – Dad won by three strokes, but Grandpa had a hole in one and everybody was amazed. Did I think of Tater even a single time? No, but I did think of Ned, because I always do.

CHAPTER 3

My class on Saturday, which is the most important day at a horse show, and also the busiest, wasn't until 2:30, so in the morning, we lazed around the house, pretending that we had all the time in the world. Mom made a coffee cake with some walnuts and maple syrup, and Joan Ariel liked it even more than I did. I could see out the window that it was foggy-moving-toward-misty, which is rare where we live, even though it's normal where we used to live. This made me even lazier – I imagined the showground covered with a blanket so thick that you couldn't see your hand in front of your face, as Grandma would say. So after the coffee cake, I went back to my room and found a book to read, *Black Gold*. I've read it twice, and I know what happens – of course the little horse wins the race – but I didn't mind reading it again. I let my eyes slide over the story and paid more attention to the pictures, especially the one of the two fillies in a match race, and overhead is a buzzard. The book says, "The buzzard is her pacemaker," which means that the little filly, the one who isn't supposed to win, decides to run as fast as a bird. I've never seen a buzzard; maybe I've never even heard that word. But I like words, and "pacemaker" made me think of that class I won – after I watched Da and then imagined him while I was riding my course, he had been my pacemaker. I decided to keep my eye on him if I got the chance. After I read for a while, I got up and got dressed like it was no big deal. Dad took me. We got to the show with plenty of time to spare, and yes, it was foggy, but just regular foggy, not woolly-blanket foggy.

Abby had already ridden in two classes and had another one to ride in just before mine, so she was all business. While I was brushing Tater, she wiped her boots down and took her hard hat off and redid her hairnet. She retied her stock, which is like a scarf that you wear around your neck, and her dad kept walking in and out, saying things like, "Be sure you sit up

straight in that far corner. Looks a little slippery to me."
When I led Tater out of the barn, I could see why he
sounded worried – the jumps were really high, maybe
four feet three inches, and now was the time that Gee
Whiz was going to prove his stuff. But since I knew
Abby's dad, I also knew that if Gee Whiz proved his
stuff and won the class, or even cleared all the jumps,
he would be for sale and would make them a lot of
money. And whether Abby wanted to sell Gee Whiz, I
had no idea.

Rodney appeared with Gee Whiz, who was stabled
in another barn, and Abby took him to the mounting
block and got on. Then he walked toward the warm-up
arena on a long rein, but he was excited – his ears were
pricked and he was looking to the left and then to the
right, as if he knew everyone was watching, and I knew
that maybe at least some people were watching, and
the better he acted, the more likely he was to be sold. I
looked at Abby. She didn't look sad and she didn't look
happy, but I know she loves Gee Whiz. This is what
my dad would call a dilemma.

Two horses went ahead of her. They must have been
from out of town, because they didn't look familiar and
neither did their riders. We get a lot of out-of-town

horses at the summer show, a few of them from Los Angeles, and Abby's dad says, "Well, good luck to them, but the fog makes them skittish, so all the better for us." His idea is that if a horse he trains does well at the summer show, then he will do well anywhere.

The first one to go ahead of Abby, a regular bay with a regular white star, did pretty well. I thought he was going to go clean until he just tapped the last rail and knocked it down, so four points off. The next one, a palomino, small and bright, started out well, but then did shy at the jump closest to the forest and deepest into the fog. A refusal – four points off. Now Gee Whiz came into the arena like he owned the place, not prancing, but on his toes. He looked around, and when he looked in my direction, I mouthed the words "Be good!"

Abby picked up the trot and did her circle, or half of her circle, because all of a sudden, Gee Whiz went up into the gallop and there was nothing she could do about it, so she headed for the first jump. She was sitting up straight, like he was going too fast, but she didn't slow him down because she didn't want to ask him not to jump. Up and over with plenty of clearance, and I said to Tater, "Close your eyes." I wanted to close my eyes, too, but I couldn't resist watching. It was like he was racing, and Abby's job was to steer the best she could. He made every jump, only touching the rail of the fourth one, a triple bar, but he did slip slightly in that wet corner, though he kept his feet. There was total silence in the grandstand and everywhere else. Abby's dad's mouth was open. We were all expecting the worst. When Gee Whiz came over the last jump, he picked up his knees so high, they went up by his cheeks, and he kicked out behind. And yes, when he came down to the trot and then the walk, he looked totally happy and proud of himself. He was ten seconds under the time limit, and so didn't win a thing, because it wasn't a race – you had to clear all the jumps and do "optimum time," which meant fast enough to go smoothly, but not too fast, because that would be dangerous. Abby's dad was shaking his head like he couldn't stop. Abby and Gee Whiz walked out of the arena on a loose rein, so I could tell he wasn't scared or wild; he was just enjoying his job a little too much.

I didn't want Tater to watch any more of this, so I rode him *very quietly* over to the warm-up, and then warmed him up – a few circles, a few transitions, two practice jumps going one direction and three going the other direction. No one came to coach me, not Abby or Jane, or even Abby's dad. I did one last canter to the left, and then Abby did come running over. She didn't say anything, but she walked me to the medium-sized arena, where our class was, and patted my leg when I was called in. And here was the pleasure of my round – nothing unexpected, just plain old Tater, looking for the jumps and jumping them. We got a fourth, not good enough to qualify for a championship class, but between you and me, I was glad. When you go into the arena to get your ribbon, you are supposed to lead your horse, and so I did, and then I led him out of the arena. I was on my way back to the barn when Da appeared on Pretty Girl. He said, "Let's go."

"Let's go where?"

"Let's go for a little ride. I'm bored."

I guess he was reading my mind.

I took Tater over to the mounting block and got back on. Tater was cool as a cucumber and didn't mind a bit. There were a lot of people around, but I didn't see Abby or Jane or my dad, and so off we went. Did I assume that Da had told someone we were going for a ride? That's what I said later, but maybe, right at that minute, I didn't think one thing or another. I just wanted to get out of the crowd.

There's a trail that doesn't lead to the beach, just wanders into the forest a ways, then turns toward the road, crosses the road, and goes through the woods for a while. It goes behind a house or two. The trail itself is wide and smooth. At first, Pretty Girl wanted to be in the lead, but then there was a loud birdcall that sort of trembled in the air, and she pricked her ears, looked around, and dropped back so that we were walking along together. I said, "Do you think that was a buzzard?"

"It didn't buzz."

I said, "Do you know what a buzzard is?"

Da said, "No."

"It's a vulture."

Da made a face.

I agreed that maybe we wouldn't want to run into a vulture in the woods. I said, "I like the word. Buzzard."

"Colonel Dudgeon loves birds. He keeps a list of the ones he sees."

Maybe Colonel Dudgeon was interesting after all.

We crossed the road. We looked both directions, and we couldn't see a single car anywhere.

I said, "Pretty Girl doesn't mind Tater." I was watching how Da sat – as if he were glued to the saddle, but graceful and relaxed.

"She's got better. Aunt Jane says she's only been here a couple of weeks, so she's settling in."

The forest got thicker and a little shadier, but if I looked up, I could see blue sky above the trees, which made me think of fog, and then Gee Whiz, and then Abby. I said, "I thought Gee Whiz really liked Abby."

Da said, "Why would you think that? Horses don't like people. They only like other horses."

"Who told you that?"

"Everybody."

We walked along. I stared between Tater's ears. I wished he would say something to me, the way Ned used to say things to me, but he never has. I wished he would turn his head and give Da the rolling eyeball that said, "You don't know what you're talking about." I wished he would show me in some way that he liked me, but he never has, except that one time when I fell off and he came over and checked on me.

I said, "Then why does Gee Whiz whinny every time he sees her coming to the pasture?"

"He thinks she's got food."

And it was true that every time, she did have a carrot or a lump of sugar.

Then I said, "When I fell off Tater last fall, he came over to see if I was okay." But as I said it, and Da smiled a little without answering, I thought that I sounded ridiculous. I said, "The trail is pretty good here. Let's trot." And so we did, around the loop that came back to the road. One car was going by, so we stood there, and then walked across and back to the barn.

You would have thought we'd been kidnapped. I looked at my watch; we were only gone for about forty-five minutes, but Jane had her hands on her hips. She glanced at me, but she stared at Da, and said, "You had better straighten up, young man!" He sat up. She said, "That's not what I mean and you know it. You may not just wander around on your own. I'm responsible for you. If anything happens to you, your mother will kill me!"

I said, "She will?" and Jane looked at me. All she said, though, was, "I thought you knew better than to disappear without a word."

And it was true that I did, so I said, "I thought Da told you." But since Da is five months younger than I am, maybe he doesn't know better. I said, "I'm sorry." But Da didn't say anything. His chin sort of stuck out, and then he dismounted Pretty Girl and walked her into the barn. To tell you the truth, I've never really seen Jane get mad, and it was a little scary. I dismounted and did my cleaning up, and then Dad took me home. The only thing he said was, "You do know better." He didn't sound angry, but he did sound disappointed.

When they brought it up at dinner, I said, "But, Dad, you told me a lot of stories about how you and that orphan you knew used to go in the woods and do things by yourselves. Did you really tell someone every time you did that?"

Dad moved his lips around, because I know that he didn't want to tell a lie.

I said, "You were eleven when you caught that beaver."

He glanced at Mom, then said, "Well, times have changed."

That's what they always say.

After dinner, we watched *The Jackie Gleason Show*. First Dad started laughing, then Mom started laughing, then Jackie pushed a pie in someone's face (a meringue pie, it looked like), so I started laughing. Then Joan Ariel, who had been looking at a book, started laughing and jumping around, and then she fell down and started crying, and by the time I finished watching her drink her bottle of milk (she only gets it at bedtime now), I was as sleepy as she was (and Mom says that drinking milk before bed makes her sleepy, too). So I went up to my room and listened for a while to the audience clapping on the TV, and to Jackie Gleason yelling (he's very loud), and then it was over.

Mom came up the stairs and put Joan Ariel in her crib, then came in to say good night to me. She kissed me, and I said, "So tell me the truth, were they the good old days or the bad old days?"

Mom started to laugh, but she saw that I was serious, so she put her hand under her chin and stared out of my window. Finally, she said, "I don't think anyone really knows. It's enjoyable to remember being young because it seems like you didn't have any aches and pains and you were always having fun, but then you remember, well, some times were hard, like for me the space of about six months when, because of the Depression, my dad lost his job, and Aunt Johanna kept having to give us money. Mom would serve the left-overs until there was nothing at all left over, and one time we had only about four small potatoes, and as soon as I complained, Dad jumped on me and asked me if I'd ever heard of the Irish potato famine, and what he told me about that was that he had ancestors who didn't even have a single potato, and so they came to the U.S. And then when I think of Aunt Johanna, I remember how sad I was when she died. So there are both good old days and bad old days." Then she kissed me and said, "These are the good old days. That's what I think when I look at you and Joan Ariel."

Did I have any good old days? Mom turned out the ceiling light. (I still had my bedside light if I wanted to read.) I tried to remember first grade, and then kinder-garten, and then nursery school, and then anything I could come up with before that. First grade was easy. I remembered Mrs. Crocker showing me how to hold my pencil and make a *K*, first the big *K*, then the little *k*, though why I remembered *K* rather than *A*, I have no idea. I remembered Mrs. Crocker's hand around mine, and me looking up at her, and her bun on the back of her head, part brown and part white. After I re-membered that, I remembered that she smelled good, and I always liked that. I thought she smelled like a blueberry muffin, though I never told anyone that and I hadn't remembered it in five years. From kindergarten, I remembered lying on the rug in front of Miss Larson, with her reading a book, trying to put us to sleep for our afternoon nap. It may be that I remembered a dream from one of those naps. There were tall windows in the kindergarten room of our school, and I dreamt that they got taller and taller and then turned into water and began to flow away. I must have said something when I woke up, because there was Miss Larson, squatting next to me, with her finger to her lips, and a smile, and she patted me on the head, and I think I remembered going back to sleep. From before kindergarten, I remembered the sandbox. I know it was before kindergarten, because it fell apart and some men came and took it away. The thing I remembered about the sandbox was what my hands looked like, making a pile of sand and then smoothing it down, and doing that over and over.

Were those the good old days for me? They didn't seem very interesting, so I thought maybe Mom was right – these are the good old days, the days of Tater and Ned and Abby, and now Da. Yup, I liked Da. He was different from all of the other kids my age, and not just because he was the only one who liked horses, and the only one who rode better than I did, and no, not because he lived a life that maybe I would like better than mine (depending on his mom and Colonel Dudgeon). Maybe it was that he seemed ready for anything.

CHAPTER 4

On Monday, I didn't have much to do. Abby always gives the horses a few days off after a show to wander around the pasture and relax. The bad thing is that sometimes an injury turns up that you didn't see, or the horse didn't reveal at the show, because everything was busy and exciting. The good thing is that you can think about what you learned and start over.

Anyway, Mom and I walked Joan Ariel over to the market on Monday, around lunchtime, in order to buy food for the week, and all the way over, I was planning how to pester her into making one of the things I really like, minute steaks with gravy and mashed potatoes followed by homemade peach ice cream, which, since

I had plenty of time, I was willing to crank. When we moved, Grandma gave us her ice-cream maker because she said it was too much work for her now. You have to pour a lot of ice and some rock salt into the tub, and then you push the container of cream and sugar into the ice. There's a paddle in the cream and sugar, and you have to turn the handle of the paddle and keep turning it until the cream and sugar freeze. If you didn't, it would turn to ice instead of ice cream.

We got to the corner. The light changed, and yes, I was talking, because I can talk and plan at the same time. I had Mom nodding at the mashed potatoes, but I hadn't got to the peach ice cream, and then I saw Ruthie Creighton in the parking lot of the store, all by herself. She was wandering here and there, as if she didn't know what she was doing, but that was the old Ruthie, not the new Ruthie, so even though I was happy to see her, I wasn't quite sure of what I was seeing. I looked her over as we got closer. She had on sneakers and socks, and the socks were pulled up. Her hair was in pigtails, and they were both the same size and positioned correctly. As we got closer, she noticed us. She smiled. I said, "What are you doing?"

"Waiting for you."

I looked around. Mom asked Ruthie how her mom and aunt were.

Ruthie said, "Mom likes her job."

"What is she doing now?"

"Bookkeeping."

I said, "I would keep a lot of books for a living," but neither one of them laughed, though Joan Ariel waved her hands.

I said, "Were you really waiting for me?"

"Yes, because I know you like to shop here and I want to ask you a question. I waited for you yesterday, too."

I said, "Don't you have anything better to do?"

"That's what I want to talk to you about."

Mom said, "I need to get Joan Ariel out of the sunshine. Ellen, I'll meet you inside. You girls step under the awning, too."

I said, "Are you ready for riding lessons?"

"No, but close. I want you to show me how to draw a horse."

"You do?"

"Yes! Look!"

She took a piece of chalk out of her pocket and

squatted down. In about ten seconds, she drew a cat, and then a fish and then a bird that looked like a robin, not a crow. She stood up. I walked around the drawings, staring at them. I said, "How did you learn to draw those?"

"Well, we have a cat, and in the spring, my aunt took me to the aquarium and let me look at the fish for most of the day, and the bird has a nest outside my bedroom window."

"Have you done any dogs?"

"There's a cocker spaniel in our neighbourhood."

"I've seen that one. It's blond."

"Have you seen the one that runs around? It's a collie. It walks down the street pretty often. Sometimes I see the owner looking for it. It's blue and white."

I said, "I wish I could see that one."

"I've made three pictures of it."

"Do you want to go to Abby's ranch with me? It isn't far away. I have a lesson Thursday."

She grinned. Then nodded. Then said, "What time?"

"About one."

She said, "I'll bring my sketch pad."

Then she walked away without a single good-bye, and it is true that that was about as much as I have ever heard Ruthie say at one time.

I stared at the drawings for a couple of minutes. I couldn't believe how fast she'd made them, and how bright they looked.

In the market, Mom was in the vegetable aisle, and sure enough, she was picking out potatoes. She had plenty of things in the cart already – butter, olive oil, French bread, which is long and thin and not sliced, some wrapped pieces of meat, a bag of flour. After the potatoes, she went to the broccoli (okay), then the cauliflower (yuck), then the carrots (hurray), then the oranges and the lemons, and then, yes, the peaches. I hadn't said a thing about ice cream, but sure enough, Mom said, "I think we should make some peach ice cream." And I stood on my tiptoes and kissed her on the cheek. We made it after dinner, and I was so tired from cranking that I fell into bed and slept like a bump on a log.

Ruthie was waiting for us on the curb outside of her house when we went to pick her up on Thursday. I had an egg salad sandwich to eat on the way, and I offered her half, but she shook her head. She didn't say a word for the whole drive, which didn't bother me – that's Ruthie. Mom tried a few remarks, but finally she looked at me out of the corner of her eye, and I shrugged a little bit, and so it was quiet. Joan Ariel wasn't with us. Mom has made friends with a woman down the street who has twins who are a little older than Joan Ariel, and sometimes Joan Ariel goes to their house and sometimes the twins, a boy and a girl, come to our house. I imagined the three of them jumping around until they triggered an earthquake, and smiled to myself.

Things were a little crazy at Abby's, and here was the reason – Jack So Far had injured himself in a race at the racetrack down south, and they had decided to send him home, and wasn't he lucky that he had a home to go to? Abby told me that Gee Whiz hardly got to go anywhere when he was racing, and when he had his injury, he had to stand in a stall for six weeks. Jack was in the round corral, looking here and looking there. He was now big, very dark, with a full tail and a high head, a real grown-up horse. When he turned and walked a few strides, I could see the sun flicker across his smooth coat and his muscles, and he did look at all the other horses like he was saying, "I'm the boss now.

I'm the boss." But I doubt whether Gee Whiz, who was up the hill in the pasture, believed him. Just then, Gee Whiz let out a screaming whinny. Abby shook her head. Ruthie said nothing. She looked straight at Jack, then went over with her sketchbook and sat down about ten feet from the round corral.

Abby said, "Is that Ruthie? Didn't you bring her to the stables once?"

"I did. Don't expect her to say anything. She wants to learn to draw a horse."

"Well, Jack is a good one to begin with."

I nodded.

But Abby still looked exhausted, and harried, as my grandmother would say, and I said, "Are you upset about something?"

"Well, I hate that Jack is injured, even though I'm glad to have him back."

"Did he break his leg?"

"No, no. Nothing like that. He did the same thing Gee Whiz did – he strained a tendon. He might get back to the track and he might not. It's not that. Dad decided to go buy some horses in Oklahoma, so I have to do all the work."

I looked around. There were five horses up the hill,

in the gelding pasture, including Beebop (the buck-ing horse), three in the mare pasture, plus Jack in the round corral and Tater and Sissy in the two stalls at the end of the barn aisle. They lived outside, too, but Abby would bring them in before our lessons. I said, "You have enough horses."

"We do, but five of them are boarders, and as for the others, nobody's buying them."

I didn't say anything about Gee Whiz, but we both looked up the hill at him, and he looked down the hill at us. Abby sighed. She said, "I guess you'd better tack up."

I went into the barn. I saw Abby walk over to Ruthie. She pointed toward the mares and the geldings, and shook her head one time, and I was sure she was tell-ing Ruthie *not* to go into the pastures by herself.

After I was tacked up and mounted and I had Tater in the ring with Abby, she said, "What do you want to do?"

She'd never asked this question before – always she's had a plan for me.

I said, "What did I do wrong at the show?"

"Not much."

"Then why didn't I win?"

"It wasn't that you didn't win, it was that Tater didn't win, because you didn't do equitation classes."

This was true. If we could only afford one class a day, I wanted to do something interesting, and, in my opinion, walk, trot, canter, now walk again, now halt, now trot to the left is not interesting. It's like taking an arithmetic test. You are almost falling asleep and you only wake up if you get an A. Hunter and jumper classes are like taking a social studies test – you have to think about what happened and who did it and why it happened, and you have all these pictures in your mind of pioneers or Christopher Columbus in the middle of the ocean or Lewis and Clark climbing the Missouri River, even though, of course, the Missouri River is flat, because it has to be in order to be a river, but there's the map and the river looks like a long hill. Even if you only get a B+, at least there was something to imagine.

"What does Tater need to do to win?"

"He needs to show off a little. Let me demonstrate." She said this in a deep voice that made me laugh. Now she turned and walked across the arena in front of me. She looked like Abby. She went maybe ten yards or so, then turned around, and when she walked back past me, she was standing up straighter, her eyebrows were lifted, she was smiling, and she was taking bigger steps as well as swinging her arms. She turned to me and said, "What's the difference?"

I thought about it for a minute, then said, "The second time, you look like you're the boss."

"That's what the judge notices."

I glanced at Jack, who was now staring toward the mare pasture. Ruthie was curled over her pad, scribbling away. When he turned and went back to his hay, she flipped the page and started scribbling again.

I said, "I don't know how Tater is ever going to look like the boss."

"Well, let's try a few things."

I turned Tater and started to walk him around Abby in a big circle. It wasn't as hard as usual, because they'd put the jumps at one end of the arena, so I didn't have to avoid them. Abby said, "Keep a light rein—"

"Light as threads."

"Yes. Now use your inside leg to push him forward, and when you feel that he's stepping under, let go of the inside rein a little bit."

I tried this three times. The first two times, nothing, and then on the third time, I did feel a bigger step underneath my inside leg, and his head dropped. I let the rein slide a little bit, and he took maybe five bigger steps before he went back to normal. I said, "I felt that."

"I could see it, too. Keep trying until you get him to take bigger steps all the way around the circle."

The more we tried it, the more I enjoyed it. Finally, we made it all the way around the circle, head lowered, bigger steps – and then, as if it was something Tater wanted to do, he went up into the trot, and the trot felt different, too. His head stayed down. Abby said, "That's the interesting thing about horses. When they're relaxed, they move forward more easily, so it's actually more fun to ride them."

I said, "This is a tune-up, then. My dad talks about that all the time."

Abby smiled and said, "Well, yeah."

I worked on this a little longer, at the walk and the trot, and then the fun part, the canter. Even at the canter, I could feel a difference – Tater seemed to be rolling more, and he was also going around his circle like he was a merry-go-round horse. We cantered both directions and came down to the walk. I said, "He likes it."

"It's relaxing."

I can see why Abby's dad and Abby herself ride horses year after year. They are always interesting, especially just after you thought they were boring. This reminded me. I said, "What was going on with Gee Whiz at the show?" I paused. "You looked scared."

She pursed her lips. "I was. But he wasn't."

"Maybe Sophia should be riding him over the higher jumps."

"Sophia made sure to tell me that."

"She could buy him."

"She has more than she can handle as it is."

Sophia is a friend of Abby's who shows a lot and, as far as I can tell, gets to have any horse she wants. She's nice, though. We walked toward the jumps. I said, "But what was going on?"

She frowned. "I don't know. You'd have to ask him."

So I did. I looked up the hill, and inside my own head, I said, "Gee Whiz, what was going on at the show?"

And he said, "The faster I go, the higher I can jump."

Up the hill, he tossed his head, as if to say, "So there."

I said, in my head, "No one agrees with you. It's not a steeplechase."

He said, "What's a steeplechase?"

I said, "A race over jumps."

And now, I kid you not, he whinnied loud and clear, as if to say, "Show me the way!"

I said, "You're too old for that."

And then he kicked up and ran across the hillside, and I didn't know what to think. I was glad that the jumping part of our lesson was just trotting over some cavalletti. I said nothing to Abby. I knew all of this was in my head, I knew I wasn't really talking to Gee Whiz, but it seemed like it, and I felt a little crazy.

Now Mom showed up beside the arena. When she drives me to Abby's ranch, she likes to go for a little walk. She says that even though she grew up in the town where we used to live, which is only twenty miles away, living here is like moving across country, and taking me to lessons at the ranch is like a vacation – she loves the sunshine and the chaparral and grass in the spring, and even the brown hills in the fall. If you went for a walk in our old town, you would be going up and down hills every step of the way. Here it is flat and then mountainous. She was also carrying her book, which she likes to read if my lesson is really long. I looked at it when she first bought it, but there weren't any horses in it, even though the title is *The Pale Horse*. I wanted to read it, but Mom says I'm too young. So of course, I want to read it even more. What will happen is that she'll finish it, and stick it in the bookcase, and I will sneak it out when she's busy and read it bit by bit. Thinking about this made me feel less crazy. Abby had me trot a few more cavalletti, but she still seemed distracted. She went out of the arena and I walked Tater here and there to cool him out. I did say to him, in my mind, "You were really good today. I think we learned something," but he didn't say anything or do anything, unless reaching his head around to shoo away a fly counts as a reply.

I also looked up the hill at Ned, and I spoke to him, too. I said, "I miss you. How are you?" But he didn't lift his head and look at me; he only swished his tail. Then I said, to myself, "Forget about it, forget about it, forget about it."

Ruthie had done seventeen pictures of Jack – his foot, his rump, his shoulder, his tail, his ears, his face from the front and the side, his hock, his knee, his eye, his nostril. She showed them to me as we were driving home. Some of them were almost finished, some of them just a few lines, but even with only a few lines, I could tell what she was trying to show. I draw pictures of horses all the time – at least, pictures of their heads. I used to get in trouble in third grade for drawing them when school got so boring that I thought I was going to fall out of my chair. I especially drew pictures of Ned's head, and I was always trying to get them right. I never did – sometimes his eye or his mouth looked like Ned, but other times, not. Ruthie's weren't like that. You could see the quickness of what she was doing right there on the page, and somehow it made the horse, which didn't look a lot like Jack, seem more alive. I told her I thought they were really good. She said, "Oh. Thanks." But she did smile when we dropped her off at her house.

As we pulled away, Mom said, "She is a strange one. But sweet."

I said, "She is a conundrum."

Mom laughed.

CHAPTER 5

After the big show, everyone needs a rest. Normally, my lessons are on Wednesday, Thursday, and Saturday – the Saturday lesson is where I help clean stalls and tack and carry bags of feed. Mom or Dad drops me at Abby's and I stay there most of the day. Lots of times I eat lunch there, which I like, because Abby's mom is a good cook.

We skipped the Wednesday lesson to give the horses their rest. My plan for that day was to go to the library and get some books, crawl under my bed and pull out everything I'd shoved there in the last two months (Mom said I had to do this), draw a few pictures of horses the way Ruthie did, and, if it got really hot, go to the swimming pool, which isn't as fun as the beach in our old town, and much further away. But if I had to make a choice between the beach and Abby's ranch, I would choose the ranch. Dad says we should get air-conditioning, but Mom doesn't like it, and they only talk about it every so often, because it's only really hot every so often.

Another thing I like to do is cross the street to the park and run around it on the sidewalk, pretending that I'm a racehorse. I got Dad to drive around the park in one of the used cars and measure it. It is four-tenths of a mile, which is just under four furlongs. The lengths of horse races are measured in furlongs. A furlong is an eighth of a mile. I did go to the library and look up "furlong." It is a really old word, and is partly made up of the word "furrow," which is the line you get when you plow a field, and partly made up of "long," of course. Just about every word is interesting, but "furlong" is especially interesting – and I think about that word every time I run around the park. Horse words are interesting, like "fetlock," "withers," "stifle," and a bunch of other names of the parts of a horse. Abby and Jane say these words as if they've never ever thought they were weird, but they are.

So, after I sat in bed for a while and thought about

words and what I was going to do all day to pass the time, I ate my breakfast, went outside, and did a completely new thing – I walked down the street toward the school and around the block that goes past Ruthie's house. And then I walked around it again. It's a short block between the middle school and the high school, and since there are a lot of playgrounds and fields, kids are over there all the time, and so, yes, I could walk around it all day long and no one would ever ask me why, except maybe Ruthie, but since she hardly says a word, she probably wouldn't ask. Maybe she would draw a picture of me.

Of course I kept my eyes and ears open, but at Ruthie's house, there was nothing to see. The shades were down (the shades at our house are down, too, to keep out the sunshine – Mom puts them up and opens the windows at night). The doors were closed. I don't think they have a car, so there was nothing in the driveway. There were two pots of leafy stems and there was a tree hanging over the front door. I didn't go up to it – from the sidewalk, it looked like a ceanothus, one of my grandmother's favourites. At our old house, there was a garden in the back that had dozens of different plants and flowers in it, and green green grass.

That was the part I hated to leave behind. Mom likes a garden, and she's working on starting one in our new yard, but she hasn't gotten very far. I kept walking. Now I sort of hopped from one shady spot to another. If the tree was big and it was really shady, I would stand there and count to twenty. When it happened, I was all the way around the block from Ruthie's house (I could see the back porch through the two yards). I was counting, and had reached fourteen. A voice said, "Tomorrow."

I looked around. There was a kid across the street, about my age, carrying a tennis racket, but he wasn't looking at me, so I didn't think he was the one who had spoken to me. I looked around again. No one. I finished counting, because I always finish what I start, and then I started walking again. I went around the block next to Ruthie's and then I went home. When I let myself in the door, Mom and Joan Ariel were tossing one of Joan Ariel's toys back and forth, something Joan Ariel likes to do, and she can catch it most of the time, which, of course, makes her laugh. Mom said, "You want some water?"

"Why?"

"It's hot. Your face is red. You look a little sweaty."

She handed me the toy, a small stuffed dog, and Joan Ariel threw her arms in the air. I tossed it. She caught it. Then she fell down like she wanted to and rolled on top of it. She said, "Bob." All of her toys are named Bob, even her Raggedy Ann doll that used to be mine.

I drank the glass of water down to the last drop, and then Mom went into the kitchen and got some pancake batter out of the refrigerator and made me pancakes. When they were cooking, she handed me a bowl of blueberries and I dropped them into the pancakes, five in each one, so twenty blueberries in four pancakes, and then she smeared each one with a little butter and stacked them and set them on the table next to the maple syrup. When I sat down, she handed me a glass of orange juice. I started eating. Out back, the trees were creaking and the shadows were flickering along the window screen. A couple of flies hit it. I wondered what book I would read that afternoon – the library is a good place to go in the summer, and it occurred to me that Grandma and Grandpa might come to dinner, and I was about to ask, when that voice said, "Tomorrow" again. And right there, as if projected onto the wall like a movie, was Ned's face turned toward me, his ears pricked, a tree behind him that looked just like one of the trees in our backyard, so I glanced out the window again, looked at that tree (a Japanese maple), and then back at the wall. No Ned.

When I used to talk to Ned in third grade, it was almost always at night, just before bed, and now I think that it was probably a dream. I'm a good dreamer. My dreams go on and on and they stick with me for a long time. Sometime in the winter, I asked Mom if she has good dreams, and she said, how would she know, she can't remember them except for an occasional image. The kids at school sometimes talk about nightmares – Mary Logan, who sat next to me in the spring, dreamt that the ceiling fan in her bedroom broke away and flew like a bird out of the window, and then she wouldn't let her mom turn on the fan for the next week even though it was hot. I overheard Jack Lawrence tell Bertie King that he dreamt that he got a new bike and then rode it down six flights of stairs. A few nights ago, I'd been looking at the atlas on our coffee table, and then I dreamt all night of flying here and there – I would see the names and then fly in close and see the landscape. The first name I saw was "Sahara," and then I floated over a gold, sandy, flat place with the wind blowing the sand into little swirls. Then I dreamt the word "Aegean" and saw a really blue ocean dotted with shiny rocks. As soon as I woke up, I knew it was a dream – it was still night, there was a little breeze blowing. I lay on my back with my eyes closed and made myself remember my dream as best I could. But back in third grade, it could have been that I didn't know the difference, really, between a dream and reality.

I finished my pancakes, scraped the last of the maple syrup off my plate with my finger, and stood up. I carried my plate to the sink, ran a little water over it, and the voice said, "Bring a carrot," which made me laugh out loud.

Nevertheless, the first thing I did when I got up Thursday morning was go to the vegetable bin and look for the two biggest carrots, and yes, as I set them on my bed next to my riding clothes, I said, "I've got 'em."

When we got to the barn, Mom parked under a tree, opened her windows, and said she was going to finish that *Pale Horse* book. I took the carrots and went looking for Abby. All of the horses were way up the hill, out of sight, except Jack, who was in the round corral, and Tater, who was staring at me from the moment

I walked into the barn, and came to the stall door. The top part was open, and he stuck his head out and whinnied, and I said, "So, is it you who's talking to me and not Ned?"

Abby said, "What?"

She stood up. She was in the stall across the aisle.

I said, "Oh, nothing."

She said, "They may not be able to talk, but they sure can communicate!" And Tater banged his knee against his door, and didn't settle down until I gave him the tip of the carrot.

We had a lesson. Abby seemed less frantic, the weather was still and warm, and the lesson was one of those good ones that you don't have to concentrate on – you can look up the hill or smell something sweet or hear a horse whinny and recognize that it is Gee Whiz or enjoy cantering around the arena, 1-2-3, 1-2-3, like a waltz, and then remember to loop, change leads, and go the other way without actually thinking about it. Maybe those are the best lessons, in some ways, because you learn that enjoying yourself is the point, after all.

Then the geldings galloped down the hill, kicking up and bucking. Ned whinnied. Abby looked up the hill. I halted Tater, who didn't care about the geldings, and looked up the hill, too.

Abby said, "What's that?"

I said, because I'm farsighted, "It's a lynx."

The lynx sashayed down the hill, then turned left and walked along below some brush. I could see the long back legs, the short tail. It paused, looked down the hill again, then ran along the hillside. It ran like a wave over the surface of the ocean. Tater tossed his head. The geldings didn't seem scared. Gee Whiz took a drink, Ned glanced up the hill, and Beebop went looking for grass or weeds or bits of hay, anything – Beebop is a great bucker, but a food horse first and last.

Abby said, "You did well today." I looked at my watch – yes, the lesson was the normal length, but it seemed to go by in a flash.

I gave Tater a long rein and he dropped his head. I said, "Did your dad get home yet?"

"Oh, he's going to be gone for another week."

"How many horses do you have to ride every day?"

"Six for now, but Da is coming to stay tomorrow."

I said, "You're kidding me." I tried not to grin.

Abby pursed her lips, then stepped up to me as if

someone could hear her secret. "Jane says he's driving her crazy. I said that we would take him on approval."

"What does that mean?"

"That we can send him back anytime. My mom likes him, though. He makes her laugh. She thinks that maybe he can't get into as much trouble out here."

"What trouble has he got into at the stables?"

"He galloped one of the horses on the golf course, he jumped into the pool with his clothes on twice, because he said he was hot, and he rode that pony, what was his name?"

"Little Bighorn?"

"Yeah. He rode him into the clubhouse and up to the bar and ordered himself a lemonade, and then he drank it, and left the glass on the bar."

"I wish I'd done that! Da is a phenomenon!"

Abby smiled.

"I have a lesson Saturday."

"Well, he has three to ride. I think your lesson is at one."

"I can get here early."

"Get here when you can, and we'll see what works out."

After I got off Tater, I untacked him, gave him the

rest of the one carrot, put the tack away, wiped him down with a cloth, and combed his mane a little while he ate his hay. Yes, I was doing everything correctly, straight out of the book, because when Abby went to the place where they kept the feed bins and the hay bales, I took the second carrot and walked over to the gelding pasture. Of course Gee Whiz was the first to meet me, and in my mind, he said, "Gimme gimme," but that was just me talking to myself. I pushed his nose away and walked along the fence. Then Beebop showed up. His ears were pricked and he snuffled a little, but he wasn't demanding anything. He said, "Please?" I kept walking, and in his Beebop way, he trotted off and leapt into the air. He had gone to rodeos in the spring. Now he was taking a break until the weather cooled off. A third horse came over, one of the boarders. I didn't know his name, but I called him Ginger because he was a chestnut. He said, "Nice to meet you." I shook my head. Now I was smiling. I got to the end of the pasture and turned around. Ned was across a little dip, up the hillside, staring at me. He looked shiny and grown-up, not so much like a puppy, and then he cantered toward me in his even, agile way, almost as smooth as a lynx. He got to the flat part by the fence and stopped on a dime, and he looked me in the eye and said, "Thank you. All they have around here are apples." I smiled, broke the carrot into four pieces, and gave them to him one by one. I petted him on the neck, which he stood quietly for, and said, "Do you remember when I got on you in the round corral and rode for a few steps?" He finished eating his carrot, dropped his nose to check the grass, then lifted his head, looked me in the eye, and bobbed his head up and down. I decided not to tell anyone about this, except maybe Ruthie, because telling Ruthie something is like putting that into a bank vault and throwing away the key.

CHAPTER 6

Saturday is Dad's big day at the Ford dealership, so I knew what I had to do. I put on my barn clothes, then heard Mom and Joan Ariel babbling in Mom's room. I was quiet as I went down the stairs. Dad was in the kitchen, drinking his coffee and reading the paper. I could see him from the hallway. I raised my eyebrows, rushed in, and said, "Oh, Daddy, can you *please* take me to the ranch? I have so much to do. Abby's dad is on a trip and Abby can't do everything herself!"

He pursed his lips and looked at his watch, then said, "Okay, but we have to leave in five minutes. Even then, I'll be late."

I grabbed two carrots out of the refrigerator and said, "I'm ready. We can leave now."

"Write your mom a note."

I did: "Dad is taking me. Please pick me up about five. Love, Ellen." I left it on the tray of Joan Ariel's high chair. I ran out the door, and Dad hurried to keep up with me. He was driving one of the used cars from the dealer – a Country Squire with something that looks like wood along the sides and enough space in the back for a pony. I had my seat belt on before he'd even closed his door, and so he laughed and was in a good mood all the way to Abby's, especially since the Country Squire just zipped along. If it hit a bump or a hole, you didn't even feel it.

He dropped me at the driveway, turned around, and zoomed off. I went through the small gate beside the big gate (it's unlocked) and got to the barn just in time to see . . .

Well, I thought I might see Da swinging from one of the overhead lights in the barn, then letting go, doing a backflip, and landing on Sissy, who would then gallop away, which would be scary but also like going to the circus, but what I saw was Da sitting on the mounting block, eating an English muffin and yawning. He said, "What time is it?"

"It's ten minutes to nine. Don't you have a watch?"

"I lost it somewhere."

"Are you driving Abby's mom crazy yet?"

"She didn't mind me pretending I was a dog when I put my hands behind my back and ate my dinner last night."

I smiled. Then I said, "Who did you ride yesterday?"

"Well, Little Bighorn came with me, because everyone else at the stables is too heavy for him, so I rode him, that mare—"

"Sissy?"

"Yeah. And Mordecai."

"I don't know that one."

"Look up the hill. See the dark bay with four white feet?"

I did.

"He's a boarder. I guess Abby's going to take him to a show and try to sell him for the owner."

I did recognize him now. He was the one who grazed with Tater sometimes, but he always backed away when I approached Tater. I said, "He's a shy one."

"It took me fifteen minutes to catch him. I guess that's why the owner wants to sell him."

"How did you catch him?"

"I took two apples, showed them to him, then offered one to your horse, what's his name?"

"Tater."

"He didn't like Tater getting the apples and him not getting them, but it still took a while, especially since after I offered Tater the apple, he was following me around like a dog because I couldn't give it to him until I caught Mordecai. Mordy's nice to ride, though." He looked up the hill again, and said, "Who's the other bay, the one to the right of Gee Whiz?"

"That's Ned."

"I never heard of Ned."

All I said was, "He's been here a while."

"He's the best-looking one of the bunch."

And Gee Whiz let out a piercing whinny.

One thing I liked about Da was that we could just talk and talk, as if we'd known each other for years.

My penalty for getting there before nine a.m. was to clean not only my own saddle and bridle but also some halters that were sandy and dusty, and two bridles, and a couple of martingales. Then I soaked all the unused bits in a bucket of water and wiped them down, saying the names to myself – kimberwick, Pelham, eggbutt snaffle, French link snaffle, curb, Tom Thumb, which Abby's dad uses on the Western horses. After that, Abby and I took Sissy and Jack So Far for a walk. My job was to go in front, leading Sissy, while Abby walked behind, leading Jack, and to hope for the best. Horses injured at the track, especially if the injury doesn't hurt too much, are ready to go go go, and you can't let them. Jack did bump Sissy one time, but she didn't do anything, and he was fine as we kept walking. After twenty minutes of walking, Abby put him in the round corral and I put Sissy in the mare pasture.

When we got back to the barn, I stood there and panted like a dog, with my tongue out, which made Abby laugh, and so we went inside and had some water and some peanut butter on crackers, which was good, and then it was time for my lesson, and what Da had been doing this whole time I had no idea, but he was smiling to himself when he joined us. Abby didn't ask him anything, and while I was tacking up Tater, he tacked up LB.

Usually, Abby has a plan for a lesson. She sees the things that I did right in the previous lesson, and also the things I did wrong, and she gets me to practise the right things and not do the wrong things. Tater also gets a lesson, because he has to learn to bend in the turn and take the proper lead in the canter and do his transitions up and down as soon as I ask him. Lessons are *orderly* and I like order. I like grown-ups to say what they plan to do and then do what they said. The other thing about order is that without order, you can't have funny things, like jokes. My dad tells jokes:

Three guys are driving in the country. One is from New York, the other is from Wyoming, and the third one is a lawyer. Late that night, the car breaks down and they go to a farmhouse and knock on the door. The farmer says he can put them up, but he only has two bedrooms, so one of them has to sleep in the barn. The guy from New York says he'll sleep in the barn. Everyone goes to bed, but pretty soon there's banging on the back door. The guy from New York says he can't sleep in the barn because the horses keep whinnying. So the guy from Wyoming says he'll sleep in the barn, but after they're all lying down, he comes banging on the door and says he can't sleep in the barn because the cows keep mooing. Now it's really late, so the lawyer

throws up his hands and says he'll sleep in the
barn. Everyone goes to bed. But then there is a
terrible racket, and the farmer goes to the back
door. It's two horses and three cows, who say they
can't sleep in the barn because now it stinks to
high heaven.

My mom and dad always laugh at this joke, which I
don't really get. The one I like is:

A horse walks into a bar. The bartender says,
"Why the long face?"

The thing about a joke is that you have to expect
one thing and then you get something else. So, yes,
our lesson was a joke.

Two ponies walk into an arena.

An instructor follows them. She closes the gate.

The instructor says, "What do you want to do?"

The boy doesn't answer.

The girl doesn't answer.

Six geldings gallop down the hill.

The pony that the boy is on rises into the air.

The boy grins, lets go of the reins, and slides off the

back of the pony and lands in the sand of the arena. He laughs.

The pony trots away, tossing his head.

The pony that the girl is on lifts his tail, drops some manure, and walks along the rail.

The instructor puts her hands on her hips, but she doesn't say, "Are you all right?" because the boy is now running around in a circle, jumping over the cavalletti and laughing. When the pony comes up to him, he pats him on the nose; then, instead of mounting with a stirrup, he throws himself into the air and lands in the saddle.

The girl on her pony understands that the other pony is very small.

The boy and his pony *mosey* around the arena.

The instructor calls out, "Pick up a nice forward trot."

The girl on her pony decides she should be ready for anything.

They trot.

They canter to the left.

They canter to the right.

The girl on the pony does a figure eight.

The boy on the pony, without being told, does a figure eight going the other direction.

The boy and the girl and two ponies weave past one another at the trot, and then the canter (with flying changes), and then the boy turns toward the rail and rises into a hand gallop.

The girl on the pony follows him.

The instructor's mouth drops open.

The girl on the pony takes the lead. She crosses the diagonal, turns left, rises into a canter, jumps a fence, comes down to the trot, turns left again, crosses the diagonal again.

The boy on the pony tries to do the same thing, but his pony refuses the jump. He does not fall off. He tries again and makes it look easy.

The girl on the pony is having a wonderful time.

The boy on the pony canters to the left, nice and slow, and just when the instructor is about to tell him to do something, he starts singing a song. The song is:

Once a jolly swagman camped by a billabong
Under the shade of a coolibah tree,
And he sang as he watched and waited till his
  billy boiled,
Who'll come a-waltzing Matilda with me?

The boy's pony canters easily and rhythmically.

The girl on the pony follows at the canter and sings along:

Waltzing Matilda, waltzing Matilda,
Who'll come a-waltzing Matilda with me?
And he sang as he watched and waited till his
    billy boiled,
Who'll come a-waltzing Matilda with me?

The instructor puts her hand over her mouth, and when the boy on the pony and the girl on the pony come to a halt in front of her, she says, "This is the weirdest lesson I ever taught." And then she adds, "I never knew I could have such a good time." And that must have been the punch line, because after that, we walked the horses out, untacked them, and put them away.

By now it was 1:23, and I remembered I was hungry. As soon as I thought that, Da said, "What's for lunch?" and Abby's mother came up behind him and said, "Tuna sandwiches," and Da was so surprised that he nearly jumped out of his boots. Then, when he saw us smiling, he did jump into the air and kept jumping like a kangaroo all the way to the house.

It turned out when we were talking over lunch that his mother was born in Australia and that his aunt still lives there on a big ranch where they have grass all year round and don't have to buy hay – they just move the horses from one pasture to another. I know that "Waltzing Matilda" is an Australian song, but Da explained to me what a billabong is (a small lake), and also a billy (a little pot) and a coolibah tree (a type of eucalyptus, which we have, too).

I said, "Why didn't your mom stay there? It sounds perfect."

"She came here when she was ten. I've only been there once, and I can hardly remember it, because I was four when I went."

"I can remember being four like it was yesterday."

"Name one thing."

I said, "One day in the fall, we came back from the market, and while Mom was putting away the groceries, I went out to the side yard and climbed a tree that was there, because Dad had left his lawn chair by the trunk. I got to the first branch and then the second, and then I looked down, and realized I was stuck, but I was afraid to get caught, so I sat there for a long time while Mom ran around looking for me. I didn't dare say a word, so she never looked up until some birds started squawking and she saw me."

"Did you get in trouble?"

"No spanking. I think I didn't get a piece of apple pie for dinner."

Da said, in his Colonel Dudgeon voice, "And so, you continued to misbehave!"

"I continued to try things out." But even as I said this, I knew I hadn't come close to trying things out the way Da did.

Abby's mom patted me on the head.

After lunch, Da told me that they were making him sleep in a stall and eat horse feed for dinner, and Abby heard this and said, "Oh, that's interesting. I thought you were staying in Danny's old bedroom. I saw your stuff in there. And as I remember, last night you ate some pork roast."

Da said, "I guess I forgot that."

Maybe so that he would remember it, Abby told us to clean the two stalls in the barn that two of the boarders lived in, and once upon a time when I was eight, this would have tired me out, but now it is easy as can be, and the manure smells like flowers. Thinking that reminded me to go out into Abby's mom's garden and look at the plants. Things were kind of spare, but there were some blossoms on the lemon tree that smelled wonderful, and there was mint and plenty of rosemary and some green beans and some agave. Oddly enough, the garden was not far from the gelding pasture, and it was amazing how I had that carrot broken up in my pocket, and so what should happen but I went to the fence, and here came Ned, and I said the word "carrot" three times, and he ate the pieces and then said, "Thank you." Then, it was very strange, the way I slipped between the fence railings (after looking around and not seeing anyone, even Da up in a tree or on the roof of the house), and I stood beside Ned and petted his silky brown coat all along his neck and his ribs and he dropped his head and flopped his ears and cocked his back hoof, and it sure looked like he fell asleep. I kept petting him for a few minutes, then sneaked between the railings again and walked along until I was going up the hill, looking for geckos and ground squirrels and little birds, like woodpeckers, and then I was on the hill where I could watch Da ride

Mordecai again, this time not having a lesson, and he did a wonderful job. I do not understand how someone five months younger than I am could do everything so well. But I decided not to be envious, because being envious is what makes the girls in my class at school fight all the time. They're best friends one day, and then one of them shows up in a skirt that the other one saw at the department store, and then at lunchtime they have a big fight about something completely different, and maybe they'll become friends again and maybe they won't. I watched and watched. He sat deep, shifted his weight side to side and backward, had a light hand, always looked where he wanted to go, kept his heels down and his shoulders straight, and was supple as a snake, and it was like that suppleness just slid down his back and into Mordecai. I thought, "Thank you, Da," but I wasn't going to say anything. I thought that the best way to be his friend was to keep teasing him and making him laugh.

CHAPTER 7

Everything was done by three. I sat on the front porch by some potted geraniums for a while and watched Abby's dog, Rusty, chase a rabbit, but pretty soon I got bored and found a book I'd left at Abby's just for this purpose, one of those books you can read over and over. I'd finished one chapter and was turning the page when Da appeared and sat down next to me. I closed the book with my finger in it and said, "When was the first time you ever rode a horse?"

He shrugged.

"You really don't remember?"

"Well, there's a picture of me sitting on a pony we had, Pirate. Mom's holding me on the pony bareback. It looks like summer, so I was about seven months old."

I dropped the book.

He said, "I was riding when I was two and a half. I remember that. She had to strap me in at first. Pirate was a small pony, under twelve hands. He was black as night, with one white snip above his nose. He died two years ago. He was thirty."

"Wow!"

"Mom says that's like ninety or more in people years. But he was trotting around his pasture and kicking up all the way to the end."

I picked up the book.

Da said, "I can't read."

"You're ten years old and you go to school. I don't believe that."

He took the book, opened it upside down, and said, "Does this sound right? 'Illufugarac nobobo et desoto?'"

I grabbed the book. He pointed at the line "She closed the carton carefully."

I said, "Were you translating that into Australian?"

We both laughed, but then he said, "I hate reading. Half the time when we have to read out loud at school, I get something wrong." Then he said, in his Colonel Dudgeon voice, "I don't understand what is wrong with that boy!"

"You've never read *Charlotte's Web*?"

He shook his head.

I ran down my list of favourites. He kept shaking his head. I was amazed. Even Jimmy Murphy has read *Johnny Tremain* and *Mrs. Piggle-Wiggle*. Da said, "So read it to me." He moved over to the other side of me, rested his back against the post, and closed his eyes. I turned to the first page and started reading.

The girl in *Charlotte's Web* might as well be me. She talks back, she loves animals, and she gets her dad to do the things she wants him to. In the first chapter, he's going to kill a runty pig, but she makes such a fuss that he gives it to her, and she feeds it with a bottle. Then her brother comes in, and he wants his own pig, of course. The whole time I was reading, I could picture myself as Fern, my dad as the farmer, and my mom, with her hands on her hips, shaking her head, as the mother. One line I read twice: "The morning light shone through its ears, turning them pink." I looked at the sun shining on the leaves of the oak tree in front of Abby's house, and could see that pink perfectly. Da was totally quiet, so when I finished the chapter, I whispered, "Are you sleeping?"

He opened his eyes and said, "Nope."

Abby came out of the front door and said, "What are you two doing?"

I said, "I'm reading my book to Da."

"Can I listen?"

I nodded. So she sat in one of the chairs and I read the second chapter, which is probably my favourite chapter, because the pig, whose name is Wilbur, follows Fern around and she loves him. Sometimes she puts him in her baby carriage with her doll, and I always think, "Why in the world would she want a doll?" I hate dolls, but she does cover him in the doll blanket, which is cute. And then her dad tells her she has to sell him, and then there was my mom, outside the gate, but I pretended not to see her. I stopped reading, though, and handed Abby the book. She took one of the geranium leaves and used it as a bookmark. I said, "How old were you when you first rode a horse?"

"Maybe three."

While Mom was driving me home, with Joan Ariel sleeping in her car seat, I was trying to remember all the things I'd been thinking about envy, because it's hard to hear about other kids having the things you want, and then there was Ruthie sitting on our lawn, and so I stopped feeling envious and started to feel lucky. She looked up when we turned into the driveway, but didn't stand. Her face was blank, which for Ruthie means sad. When Mom stopped the car, I jumped out and ran over to her. Maybe I was a little too loud. I said, "Have you been waiting long? Sorry, I was gone all day. It's hot, you must be hot. You want to come inside? You want to have a glass of water?"

She kept looking at me. I held out my hand, and she took it and stood up. Okay, she rose without even putting her other hand on the grass. Another thing to envy. Ruthie used to be smaller than I am, but now she's maybe three inches taller, and even so, she could launch herself like that. I took her in through the front door, went to the kitchen, got us both glasses of water. She took hers and stared at it, then drank some. Right then, I knew she had a secret, but when she opened her mouth, she said, "Can I draw some of the flowers in your garden? Leaves and branches, too. We don't have a garden, and I know you do."

I said, "Sure."

She said, "Do you have any paper?"

And then I decided that her secret, or part of her secret, was that her family was back to having no money. I went over to Dad's desk and opened the bottom drawer. I gave Ruthie some of Dad's typing paper. She did have her pencils, and they were sharpened. We walked through the kitchen and out into the back, which is fenced and shady, but it gets enough sun for Mom's garden. Ruthie walked here and there, drawing a daylily or two. Then she sat down in front of Mom's favourite, the lemon tree, and drew the whole thing – the few little blossoms, the hanging lemons, the leaves, the pot, which is big. When she stood up, I said, "Smell the blossoms. They are the *best*." So she did. I was happy. I've always liked it when Ruthie does what I tell her. When we went back through the kitchen, Joan Ariel was in her high chair, playing with a string bean and a few peas – she was holding the string bean in her left hand and using it to push the peas here and there. Ruthie looked at her as if she was thinking about drawing a picture of her, but then Mom turned from the stove and said, "You want to stay for dinner?" and Ruthie's face went red and she shook her head and turned toward the living room. She was like an animal who wanted to escape. I imagined her digging a hole beneath the door like a dog, then wiggling under and running off, but when I opened the door, I just said, "Come back anytime."

At dinner, Mom said, "She looks like she's made of sticks now."

Dad said, "I thought they were doing better."

Mom said, "I did, too. You never know."

I said, "How can we find out?"

Mom said, "No idea. I don't know their friends, if they have any. You know, when we were living in the old place, that constant gossip drove me crazy, but I guess it has its uses."

That night, I went to bed early, right after Joan Ariel went to bed. It wasn't even dark. Since it had been a warm day, my window onto the backyard was wide open, and I could hear the birds rustling in the trees and sometimes calling. I also heard an owl, quiet and far away, hooting. A car would go by and drown out the owl, and then it would be quiet again, and there was the owl. In my mind, I thought, "Owl, owl, fly over to Ruthie's, then fly back and tell me what's going on." When I remembered my long day, the thing I remembered most clearly was standing on the hill above the gelding pasture, watching Da ride. You can see a lot if you just keep looking.

The next day, we went back to our old town and went to church with Grandma and Grandpa. We do that every couple of months, mostly because we haven't found a church everyone likes in our new town. Dad actually doesn't like church at all, and Mom keeps her mouth shut. It used to be that every time we went to church, Joan Ariel would start screaming after about ten minutes, but I don't mind church, especially Grandma's church, because the choir is very good, and sings a lot of different songs. It's sort of like putting on a record, only sometimes it's better. And after church, there's always dinner at Grandma's. The funny thing is that you don't have to try anything new on Sunday – it's always roast chicken and mashed potatoes or beef stew, with a peach pie afterward. I think that Grandma loves to make a really big dinner so that she'll have lots of leftovers for the next few days. This time, we had goulash and noodles, and even Joan Ariel sucked it right down. We got home about four. Joan Ariel had been up since five a.m., so Mom went to take a nap and Dad took Joan Ariel out into the backyard and set her in her outside playpen, and what did I do? Well, I took a walk. I told Dad I was going to have a little run around the park to see if I've got any faster, and as soon as I used the word "furlong," he laughed and said, "She's off!"

Since I cannot tell a lie, I did take a run around the park – it was full of kids who kept getting in my way – and then I veered off and headed toward Ruthie's house. There weren't as many people on the street because it was hot. I walked around Ruthie's block, just like I'd done before, and looked at her house from the front (I was across the street, under a tree) and from the back, through the neighbour's yard. I thought there might be something going on, since it was Sunday, but just like the last time, there was nothing. The shades were drawn, the driveway was empty, the grass in the tiny yard wasn't even brown – what few bits there were lying in the dirt. No wonder she had to come to my house to look for flowers and leaves. And lemons. I should have given her a lemon. Just to make sure, I walked over to the junior high, then back again and around Ruthie's block. Still nothing. Of course when I got home, Mom was fit to be tied, or so she said. What was I . . . Why didn't I . . .

I saw Dad smiling behind her. She shook her head and threw up her arms and we had cold potato soup for dinner, then lime Popsicles, which for a hot day was plenty.

Everything was steamy and quiet for the next

couple of days. We went to the swimming pool, and even Joan Ariel got to swim – Mom walked around in the shallow end and held on to Joan Ariel while she smacked the water with her hands and kicked her feet. Mom and Dad are both big believers in teaching kids to swim as soon as possible. By the time I was three, I had one of those bubbles that keeps you afloat, and by the time I was four, I could swim across the pool, though I wasn't allowed in the deep end. I am sure that Da was already jumping off the high board when he was two, and scaring the pants off his mom, but I didn't do that. Even when Joan Ariel is in the bathtub, Mom tells her to kick and paddle. The bubble is too big for her right now, but she's not the one who is going to stare at Mom and then run into the pool just to be naughty.

So there I was, Tuesday night, sitting in the living room, bored to death, when I went over to Dad's bookcase and took out one of his books. It was about a guy named Sherlock Holmes, whom I'd heard of, and because of that I leafed through it, and there was the word that always pulls me in, "blaze" as in "Silver Blaze." It was a story about a horse.

It took me a while to get used to the way it was

written – all very stiff and with a lot of big words, but lots of old books are like that, and if you keep at it, pretty soon you understand, even if you have to skip some of the words or look them up. Words are interesting, anyway, and one I liked in "Silver Blaze" was "blunder." It means "mistake," but the sound of it makes you laugh. Another was "surmise," which is a guess. I guess about things all the time, so I surmise that I will have to say "I surmise" all the time. Anyway, I was disappointed at first because there wasn't much about the horse – he wasn't anyone's friend. But then there was poison and a dead body and a big empty beautiful place called Dartmoor, so I kept reading, and even though when I read Nancy Drew, I sometimes understand what's going on before I get to the end, Sherlock Holmes surprised me over and over, and so I liked it. At one point, Sherlock and his friend, who is telling the story, start walking late in the afternoon out into the empty area, and because it's muddy, pretty soon they see the horse's hoofprints in the mud, and that tells them where he was going. Then Sherlock says this: "See the value of imagination. It is the one quality which Gregory lacks. We imagined what might have happened, acted upon the supposition, and find ourselves justified. Let us proceed." Or, as I might say, "It's worth it to make things up, because you could turn out to be right." What I did say, out loud but quietly, was, "Are you listening, Ned?" Anyway, I followed the story all the way to the end – it wasn't that long, and every few paragraphs, Sherlock surprised me a little bit, but then when I got to the end, after the race, and Sherlock told how everything had happened and why, I understood it backward, you might say, and I think that's what life is like. One example is how when Mom and Dad told me that we were going to adopt a new baby, and then, after that, that I was adopted, I was so amazed that I didn't have a word to say, which is a once-in-a-lifetime experience for me, and then I got used to the idea, and then I saw why I don't look like any old pictures of Mom or Dad but love them anyway and know they are my family.

I put away the book and went upstairs. It was still hot, but there was a little cross-breeze, and I could feel the temperature going down. I changed into my summer pyjamas and slipped under the sheet. Then, as it got darker, I closed my eyes and imagined Tater and Ned. Tater was by the fence rail, dozing, and Ned was staring here and staring there, trotting, then cantering, then trotting, then taking a drink of water, then trotting some more. Gee Whiz was tossing his head, and then he whinnied, and his whinny said, "Hey, kid, relax!" But Ned kept trotting back and forth. Was it coyotes or rabbits or snakes or nothing at all? I couldn't tell. Then I said, "Ned, go to sleep." I said it out loud, in a soft voice. I imagined it. I hoped I would find myself justified.

CHAPTER 8

On Wednesday, I went to Abby's a little early. When Dad dropped me off, I ran up the driveway to the house. Abby's mom was sweeping the front porch. I shouted, "Hi!" and when she looked up, I tried to be extra observant, in order to see if she looked haggard or worn out because of Da, but she looked fine. I wondered if maybe they locked him in his room at night just to keep him out of trouble, but I didn't say anything. I ran around the house to the barn, took off my sweater, and set down my carrots. The very thing that I had imagined was happening – Da was in the arena, walking Mordecai, and Abby was brushing Ned. Ned lifted his head and looked at me when I came into the barn. I said, "Are you getting on or are you finished?"

"Just getting on," said Abby.

"Why don't you look happy?"

"Don't I? Well, he nearly dumped me yesterday. Everything was fine for a long time, and then he grabbed the bit and his head shot into the air, and he ran off. He didn't buck, but he almost got out from under me. I thought I had him figured out."

She kept brushing with the soft brush, which Ned likes (which they all like), and he dropped his head again. What popped out of my mouth was, "Let me get on Sissy and ride with you."

"How long can you stay?" Then, "I thought you didn't like Sissy."

I said, "Well, I haven't ridden her in a long time. I just want to try again."

"Sure. She could stand the work."

So I went to the mare pasture and watched the mares. There were four of them out – Sissy, Delilah, Darleen, and Blanche. Delilah and Darleen are boarders, both Western horses that Abby's dad trains, and Blanche is a three-year-old black quarter horse who is just starting to be ridden. I heard Abby's dad say that she could go either way (English or Western) depending on how big she ends up being and her length of stride. Sissy didn't come to me, but she also didn't stare at me then trot away as if she were saying, "Uh-oh, you again." After I put her halter on and led her to the gate, she walked along behind me, and I didn't imagine her saying, "Torture." Some horses like to be ridden, just to have something to do and a way to get out into the world.

Sissy wasn't very dirty, and Abby helped me tack her up while Ned stood in the cross-ties, pawing. Then we led them out to the mounting block and got on. I didn't tell Abby what I was imagining, which was that with Sissy nearby, Ned would be a good good boy, but I did imagine it when we were walking to the arena, Ned in the lead and Sissy, her head down as if she were almost asleep, right behind him.

We had a lesson, but it was a "pay attention" lesson rather than a "do this" lesson. While we were walking, I paid attention to Da and Mordecai. They were doing an exercise where they trotted down the long side, along the fence, then made a big loop away from the fence without slowing or speeding up. Then Da would straighten Mordecai, trot a few steps, and get him to step sideways until he was along the fence again. Then he would trot to the other end of the long side, turn the other direction, and push Mordecai toward the fence. Mordecai looked like he was doing a dance like they do in the movies, where they cross their legs and tap their toes. I said, "Is he going to rear up and spin around?"

Abby laughed. She said, "They're doing Jane's favourite exercise. It's called a leg yield."

"How do you do it?"

"You have him bend around your inside leg as if he's making a circle, but instead of making the circle, you continue down the rail. After they've done it for a while, their backs get flexible and they do everything more easily."

I tried this with Sissy. She said, "What in the world are you talking about?" exactly in my grandmother's voice.

I said, "Would Sissy do that?"

"We've never worked on that. We should, though. It takes some training. When I give you your lesson, you can try it with Tater, and then sometime, when you understand what it feels like, you can try it on Sissy."

We walked quietly around the arena, doing a few circles, crossing the diagonal, going down the centre line. Either I was stronger, or Sissy was more willing, because she was easier to ride than she had been, and the pleasure was that her stride was bigger than Tater's and sort of bounced me along. I stayed fairly close to Abby and Ned – in the vicinity, you might say, but not being a pest. What I observed was that Ned's gaits were even more smooth than they used to be, what I surmised was that Abby had succeeded in teaching him to balance himself, and what I imagined was that he was comfortable in Sissy's presence. When we were finished, Abby was happy with both of them. I didn't say anything, because Sherlock Holmes would surmise that one time doesn't count for much.

Da wasn't saying anything, either. He brought Mordecai to the barn, untacked him, washed him a little where he was sweaty from the saddle, then walked him out of the barn to the turnout and came back with LB. He put him in the cross-ties and started currying him. Abby went back to the hay barn. I said, "You're all business today."

Da shrugged.

"What's the matter? Are they locking you in your room at night?" Actually, I did not want this bit of imagination to turn out to be true.

"No, as if that would work anyway. I'm sad that I'm so stupid."

"What are you talking about?"

"The reading thing. I realized after we talked about it that Mom didn't hold me back because I was young, she held me back because my teacher in kindergarten told her to. Her name was Miss Livingston. I had to do kindergarten twice, and then I was terrible in first grade. Maybe I wasn't joking when I said that I can't read. I found that book of yours, and I tried the first two chapters, and they didn't make any sense at all."

"You must have never known anyone with a pet pig."

"I did, though. A friend of my mom's. He had it for four years and it got to be eight hundred pounds."

"Was it as big as a pony?"

"Shorter but wider. The kids would ride it around the yard. They called him Spiffy. They brushed him like a horse, and he liked it. Pigs aren't dirty like in that book."

I didn't know what to say. We finished tacking up and led the ponies out of the barn. I took Tater to the mounting block and Da mounted LB from the ground, though he didn't throw himself up. Abby was now in the house, so we ambled into the arena and walked around on a loose rein. Da started talking again. "Do you have anything else you could read to me?"

"Do you know about Sherlock Holmes?"

"My mom likes those movies. There's one that comes on the late movie sometimes called *The Hound of the Baskervilles*. She always says that if she'd had the chance, she could have trained that dog. They just didn't use the right techniques."

"Well, the movies started out as stories. I have one of those books at home, and can read you a couple."

"When?"

"Tomorrow."

We picked up the trot just as Abby came into the arena and closed the gate. Now it was my turn to learn. I went up to Abby and said, "I want to do everything that Da does. I want to observe him" – I emphasized the word "observe" – "and then imitate him."

"You always make me laugh."

Da came around the triple that was in the centre of the arena. I turned Tater and trotted after him. And I truly hoped that Da would not get LB to rear up so that he could slide off his back end. That was something I did not want to imitate.

I guess Abby had decided that there should be those leg yields, and Da was good at that. After we were warmed up, I watched Da do four leg yields at the walk, two in each direction, then I did my best, but Tater pretended not to know anything about leg yields, so the next thing I did was ride Tater right behind LB and watch what Da did with his legs, his hands, and his seat. What he did was put the outside leg behind the girth and the inside leg on the girth, open his inside rein a little, and shift his seat to the outside. Then he urged LB by prodding him with his heels, and pretty soon, LB was crossing his outside hind leg in front of his inside hind leg and moving along the rail even though he was not turned toward the rail. I tried it again, doing what Da had been doing, and it worked—Tater moved along the rail and I could feel his hind legs crossing. We did it a few more times at the walk, and then at the trot. The interesting thing was that Tater perked up while we were doing it, and moved along very nicely. Then we did it on a circle, out and in, out and in, both directions. Now they were warmed up, so we cantered around the arena a few times while Abby lowered the triple, and then we did the jumping part.

There are pairs classes in some horse shows – my favourite is pairs abreast, where the riders wear all their fanciest clothes, and the two horses, who look like one another, go around the course together. The winners are the ones who seem glued to each other, and who do *not* switch their tails and pin their ears the whole time, because the horses have to like one another. Da and I did our jumping like the other kind of pairs class, where one horse follows the other one about four lengths behind, and then the first horse drops back and the second horse goes in front. We did it twice, and I started out behind. It was a good way to see Da's balance close up, to see how he rose and went forward as LB began to jump the fence, just as easy as you please, the way a branch might lift in a breeze – the most normal thing in the world. When he slowed down and it was my turn to take the lead, I went around him to the right and I did that thing I do so well, which is to think of two things at the same time – the jump coming up and the sight of Da rising to meet the jump. Then Abby let us do pairs abreast over the two oxers on the long side. Tater is bigger than LB, so I had to sit up a little to get him to slow down, and Da had to push a little to get LB to lengthen his stride. The first time, Tater was in front by a head, and the second time, going the other direction, LB was a little in front, let's say half a head, but the third time, Tater was light as a feather, and we seemed exactly together. Afterward, Abby said that over both oxers, their front knees rose and bent at exactly the same time, and even their ears were pricked in the same way. Then she told us about going to a show a few years ago where there was a pairs abreast class, and the horses that won looked exactly alike except that one had a white left foot and the other had a white right foot, no other markings, and the riders held each other's reins – and the rider on the left held both left reins and the rider on the right held both right reins – and the riders' legs were almost touching.

I said, "Was that the Goldman twins?"

"No, but they were there, and they wanted to do it. It looked dangerous to me, but nothing looks dangerous to them."

"Do they still take lessons?"

"They did last summer, but this summer, they're in France, studying French. That friend of theirs from France talked them into it."

I said, "I'm surprised she had to."

Abby said, "My guess is, she mentioned it, and they bought the tickets." Then, "You know, they also have hunt teams, where three horses jump abreast."

Da said, "My mom and Aunt Jane used to do that with a friend of theirs."

I said, "Am I surprised? They've done everything."

Da said, "When you're foxhunting, lots of people go over the fence at the same time, or almost the same time, especially the whippers-in."

I said, "What—"

Da said, "Those are the ones who make sure that the hounds stay together, but they have to be in front so that the hounds don't run away from them."

I said, "Do you like foxhunting?"

"I like drag hunting, but I don't like the hounds killing the fox. Mom says, 'Well then, why are you not a vegetarian?' and I say, 'Because you would starve me to death if I were,' and so we don't talk about it."

I said, "Let's have one last little canter." I turned, went to the rail, and rose into a very nice canter on Tater's not-so-good lead, his right, and Da was close behind me. Then I circled a jump, and got behind him, and he went on, around and around, across the diagonal – Da, flying change; me, simple change – and then around to the left. And then it was hot, so the ponies were sweaty, and we walked up the hill and back down to cool them out.

I could see Ned in the pasture, all by himself. Gee Whiz and Beebop were eating the last of their hay together, and so were two of the boarders who I didn't know. When those two trotted toward Ned, he spun around and trotted away. I said to Tater, "Are you Ned's friend?" And Tater tossed his head toward LB as if to say, "My friend is right here."

On the way home, I asked Mom what a vegetarian was, and she told me that it was a person who didn't eat meat, though they might eat eggs and cheese. We were almost to our house when she said, "Grandma was a vegetarian, but Grandpa said he wasn't going to stand for it, so she went back to eating meat. What I think is that when the husband is a vegetarian, everybody is, but when the wife is, nobody is."

When we had dinner that night, I watched Mom and Dad, both. Mom ate some of a chicken breast, Dad ate both legs, and Joan Ariel would only eat the mashed potatoes and the mashed peas, so I guess she was making her opinions known. I ate like Mom and then I thought about it for the rest of the evening, so much that I almost forgot to put the Sherlock Holmes book with my barn clothes, but I remembered when I was almost asleep, then got up and went downstairs in the dark. It was right there by the sofa. I carried it upstairs, and the only light was the moonlight flickering through the tree over the house. The fact is, the older you get, the more things there are to think about, and I don't know if that's a good thing or a bad thing.

CHAPTER 9

Dad was ready to take me early again, which was fine with me, and with Mom, too, since she wanted to go visit Grandma and Grandpa and get Joan Ariel out of the heat. Back in our old town, you can wander in the parks near the lighthouse all summer, and you have to remember to bring a sweater along. Dad drove me in a used car he was trying out, a VW Microbus, or so he said, and riding in it was like being inside a bubble and floating down the river. He said that there are some people who just live in one of these and drive around the country, and I thought, "Well, why not, if you have enough books." I could tell he *respected* it, but he didn't like it much, and maybe because it was like Sissy, willing to go, but not to go fast.

We did finally get there. Sissy was part of my plan for the day, but I hadn't quite figured out how to make it work. Da was lying under a tree with his hands beneath his head and his eyes closed. He said, "Hey, Ellen," without even opening them.

"How did you know it was me?"

"By your step. You always sound like you're in a hurry."

And I am. I said, "Good deduction."

"What's a deduction?"

"That's when you put two and two together and come up with four. But they have to be good twos."

He laughed and sat up, then said, "Abby and her mom went into town to do some things."

"Have you eaten them out of house and home?"

"I tried."

"Do you have a big appetite?"

"Yeah. I'm like my dad, I guess. He was under five feet tall until he turned fifteen, and then he grew a foot in a year. Eventually he got to six feet four. He still loves to eat."

I said, "Where's your dad?"

"He's at home, but he works all day and all night,

so Mom thought it would be easier for me to stay with Aunt Jane."

"Abby's mom is a good cook."

He saw the book.

"Read me a story."

I'd been planning to read the story about a speckled band, but when I just opened the book, there was the first page of *The Hound of the Baskervilles,* and so I started reading. Da leaned forward so he could hear every word, and he paid close attention.

We could picture Sherlock eating breakfast and Watson picking up some kind of stick, and the two of them talking about it, but there were a lot of words that I had to repeat: "hearth-rug," "bulbous," "souvenir," "ferrule," "piqued." But I kept going and we did understand that Watson has a lot of ideas that Sherlock disagrees with, and Sherlock is sort of making fun of him, even though Watson is a doctor and Sherlock's best friend. Right after I got to the word "mastiff," and said, "What is a mastiff?" and Da said that a mastiff is a big dog, about as tall as a Great Dane but much heavier, with a droopy face and floppy ears, Abby and her mom drove through the gate. Abby jumped out, and then her mom came over and told us that we must be hungry, and even though it was only eleven, of course we were, because I could see that she had a bag from the bakery in her hand, and that turned out to be full of blueberry muffins, and so we forgot about the hound and deduction and only imagined how delicious those muffins were going to be, and we were right.

The muffins put Abby in a good mood, too, and so when I said, "I think we should do Ned and Sissy again," she nodded, and so we did. We started out in the arena. I did what Abby told me, but I also tried my own experiment, which was to get Sissy closer to Ned, then further away, then closer, then further away. At one point, Sissy and I were between Ned and the railing. His head was down and he seemed relaxed, just walking along. I stepped her over to the railing and asked for the canter, and we eased off. I turned and looked at Ned, but even though he'd lifted his head, he was just looking. At the far end of the arena, we looped around a jump, and the whole time I was watching Ned. He was still walking, but he was also not relaxed. He kept looking at us. I cantered down the centre of the arena, then turned, came down to the walk, and joined them again.

Abby said, "Why did you do that?"

"I wanted to see if Sissy could canter away and stay even." And I did want to see that, but mostly I wanted to see if Ned cared. He cared. In my own mind, I heard Ned say, "Don't do that again."

And in my own mind, I said, "You have to be by yourself sometimes."

He tossed his head and said, "I don't want to be. I'm a herd animal."

I couldn't help smiling at that one. As we walked along, I said, "You have a herd."

Ned said, "You mean, all the geldings? That's not a herd – that's a gang."

I said, "What's the difference?"

"A herd sticks together and a gang pushes you around."

I was surprised Ned knew this. I thought that was the definition of fifth grade. I said, "You can stay out of the way. That's what I do."

"But then you're by yourself all the time."

Abby said, "Are you asleep with your eyes open? I asked you twice if you wanted to jump a little bit."

"Was my jaw hanging?"

Abby laughed. "No."

"Then I must be thinking about stuff. I don't want to jump Sissy. Can we do one thing and then go for a trail ride?"

"Sure, what?"

"That weaving thing where we trot along the rail and crisscross one another."

"We can try. But you have to get Sissy to move up, because Ned's trot is quicker than hers."

I went over to one of the jumps that had wings on each side and took the crop that Abby leaves there on the crossbeam so that you can grab it without dismounting. I didn't hit Sissy with it, but I flourished it a little, and she perked up. We went to the end of the long side, stood Ned and Sissy about five feet from one another, with Sissy on the outside, and started our trot. The outside horse crosses first, so I crossed, then we trotted four steps, then Ned crossed, then four steps, then Sissy, to the end of the arena. I didn't have to smack Sissy, and I could keep my eye on Ned. His trot is beautiful, his body is supple, he steps forward behind – all of that is regular Ned. What I cared about was that neither he nor Sissy pinned their ears even once, he seemed relaxed, Abby's reins were light as threads, and Sissy didn't switch her tail. We did it one more time, also good, and then we walked out of the arena just as Da was coming over. I said, "We're going up the hill. Want to come along?"

"Sure." He turned to follow Sissy. Ned was in the lead. As soon as Mordecai followed Sissy, Ned said, "I don't want to be in front." I waited for Sissy to say something, but she didn't. I waited for Mordecai to say something, but he didn't. I decided that I can't imagine Sissy and Mordecai well enough to draw any conclusions about them. I said, "Try it. Step by step."

I kept my eye on Ned's haunches and on his ears, which I could see as he turned his head to look here and there. Abby had him on a loose rein, but she was alert, too, and I could tell that if she sensed that he was ready to misbehave, she would take hold of him. I said, in my own mind, "Easy, easy, easy." We continued up the hill. They all had to put their heads down, because that's what horses do when they climb hills. We leaned forward. It was an effort. Ned liked it, because he had to pay attention, Sissy didn't like it, because she's lazy, and Mordecai didn't care, because he just likes to move.

From the top of the hill, we could see Jack in the

round corral, having a roll, the mares in the shade down by the creek bed, Abby's mom with her hands on her hips, staring at the lemon tree, and the geldings. They were quiet, finishing their hay. Then Gee Whiz started wandering along the fence line with his head down, like he was looking for chamomile or something (though it's late in the year for chamomile), and Bee-bop lay down and began to roll. At that very moment, like he knew he was stealing, one of the boarders trotted over to what was left of their pile of hay and began eating it. Gee Whiz squealed, stormed up the hill, kicked out at the boarder, who ducked to the side and trotted away. Ned said, "See?"

I said, "Gee Whiz just wants you to behave properly."

Ned said, "According to his rules."

Now we came to the trail that runs along the side of the hill. Abby turned Ned to the left and picked up the trot. Da and I followed — and truly, there is nothing like being out in the world on a horse and moving right along on a loose rein, looking at the golden grass and the dark oaks, and having a hawk float by with his wings spread, quiet as a mouse, and then feeling a breeze that seems to have come over from the ocean, cool and moist. We went up and up, and then stopped to look around at the other hills that belong to the Jordan Ranch, which is huge.

I said, "How's Ned feel about being the lead horse?"

"Not happy, but willing."

I didn't volunteer. We walked back the way we came, a little more carefully, which you do when you're going downhill, and I watched the geldings some more. Someone else was watching them, too, and that was Jack So Far. He stared at them and whinnied, pawed, tossed his head, trotted the circle of the round corral waving his tail. I said, "Jack seems ready to get out there."

"Confinement is driving him crazy. But the vet says another week. He was on a tranquillizing drug, but we weaned him off that."

"Is he going to get along with Gee Whiz?"

Abby said, "I hope so. He did before."

Ned said, "No."

I said, "I thought Gee Whiz was for sale."

"Of course he is. Someone came to look at him after the show. They're coming back next week." She sighed. "The trainer thinks he has potential. He shows down in L.A., in the big shows. Since Gee Whiz raced down there, he's used to the weather and the heat."

"Why didn't they just buy him?"

Abby didn't say anything, and in my mind, Ned said, "Dontcha wonder. Ha."

Now Da piped up. I'd practically forgotten him. He said, "You should show him to Colonel Dudgeon. His whole life is buying and selling show horses. And" – in his Colonel Dudgeon voice – "I know what I'm doing and don't you forget it, young man!"

We laughed. Ned seemed calmer heading back to the barn.

Later, during our lesson – me on Tater and Da on LB – I kept my mouth shut. Since Da likes to talk, he would ask Abby questions even when she was telling us to circle at the walk, then the trot, then the canter. It was like riding came so naturally to him that he didn't have to think about it, so he could keep on talking even when he was doing just the right thing (and LB was, too). He asked her about Jack's racing record, about how much money he won, about his breeding (that is, his sire and dam), about who trained him and who broke him, and all of that. She told him about how Jack was orphaned as a foal and how sad that was. As for me and Tater, we were like the quiet kids in the back of the classroom who keep our eyes open and do what the other kids are doing. Every so often, Abby would tell me to lift my hands a little or put my outside leg back a little further to get Tater to step over behind. Or she would tell me my canter depart was good. But mostly, she and Da talked about Jack, which was fine with me, because, since Tater was being very good, I kept my eyes on the gelding pasture.

Ned was exactly right. We had given them their noon hay, which is grass hay, not very exciting. For a while they ate; then for a while they argued. One of the boarders chased Ned away from his hay, then trotted back to his own hay. Mordecai kept his eye out. He's small, so the others bothered him, too, but he didn't seem to care, though when one of the boarders came too close, he leapt forward and kicked out with both hind legs as if he really meant it. That boarder trotted away. Abby and Da kept talking. It was like I had instructed Da to distract Abby so that I could *proceed with my investigation* into why Ned didn't like the other geldings. The mares had come up from the creek and were eating their hay, too, but nothing. Just nothing. They ate. That was all.

Da said, "What's the most number of times you ever fell off in one day?"

Abby said, "Once."

Da said, "I fell off four times in one day when I was seven."

"Because you asked the horse to rear up four times, and then you slid backward?"

"No. I only just learned to do that."

I said, "Why bother?" I threw myself off a pony once to show Mom that falling off isn't that bad, to get her to let me take jumping lessons, but it did hurt (elbow and wrist), though I kept that to myself.

He didn't answer. He said, "They were real falls. Mom was giving me a lesson."

I said, "My mom says little kids bounce."

"Well, I didn't bounce. I sort of flopped. That makes the landing easier."

I tried to understand what this meant, and then he showed us. He got Mordecai to trot toward the gate, then dropped off like a rag doll and landed on his back. Mordecai trotted two more steps, then halted, looked around, and headed for the grass that grew along the edge of the arena. Da jumped up and went to catch him, but Mordecai wasn't having any of that – he tossed his head and trotted away. It took ten minutes to catch him, and we only managed to do it after Abby went and got some oats in the bucket. When Da was back on him, I said, "I guess you learned your lesson, huh?" and Da said, "Never." We both laughed. I realized that I liked Da because he showed me lots of new things, including ones I would never dare try.

CHAPTER 10

Egg salad sandwiches and Gravenstein apples for lunch, and the Gravensteins, of course, got me talking about Grandma's apple pies, which are best with Gravensteins. They come from around here and ripen in the summer, which means that since you haven't had an apple pie in a really long time, it's the only thing you could possibly want for dessert, and that includes chocolate cake. Abby's mom said that she'd always wished for some apple trees, then we talked about apple names – pippin, russet, Pink Pearl, Arkansas Black. Abby's mom said that her favourite was Lord Peckover, and Da said that his mom had one of those trees. After lunch, it was already two and it was hot hot hot. I kept my eye on Da, and went over to the bookcase, where I had left the Sherlock Holmes book, and then I sniffled and sighed and made some other noises as I walked through the room, out the door, and over to the shade of the big tree. I looked at my watch. It took Da six minutes and four seconds to find me.

I already had the book open, but since I didn't want to read ahead, I was looking around and of course over to the gelding pasture, where Gee Whiz whinnied three times. Then Jack, in the round corral, whinnied back three times. The first thing Da said when he sat down was, "Colonel Dudgeon better find a home for the grey, because I think there is going to be a big fight if Jack gets turned out with the other geldings."

"Abby's dad says that Jack and Gee Whiz will work it out once they're turned out in the same pasture."

"But if you have two talented horses that could sell for a lot of money, I don't think you want them to work it out."

And Ned said, "Yes."

I read for maybe half an hour – until the shade of the tree slipped away from us, and we were squinting in the sunshine. I started where the man who owned the "stick" returns and brings a "manuscript," which he reads aloud in a "high, cracking voice." I tried to do the same thing. At first Da was grinning, but then I saw him close his eyes and pay attention. The manuscript is about a very bad man named Hugo from the old days, who kidnaps a girl, and she escapes by climbing down some ivy and running home, "there being three leagues betwixt the Hall and her father's farm." I said, "I wonder how far that is."

Da said, "I think a league is about three miles."

"How would you know?"

"My grandfather uses that word, and once I asked my mother what it meant." He closed his eyes again.

I read the rest. The bad part was that this Hugo swore that he would give himself over to the powers of evil if he didn't catch the girl, and then a shepherd told his friends that he had seen Hugo's hounds, and then Hugo on his "black mare" going after the girl, and then another hound, much bigger and scarier, silently chasing Hugo and the mare. They found Hugo, dead on the ground with his throat torn out.

I put my finger on the page, and said, "Do you think it's okay if we read this?"

"You've read 'Little Red Riding Hood,' right? Or 'Hansel and Gretel'? What's the difference?"

I said, "Okay. But what I want to know is what

happened to the mare, and what she thought about all of this."

"If he was that bad of a person, I'm sure she thought she was better off, especially if for the rest of her life she was free to gallop around on the moor."

I then read the next part, which was a newspaper article about the death Sherlock is supposed to *investigate,* in my flat newspaper voice. After that, the man who is visiting Sherlock tells him the "private facts," and the most important of them is that right by the man who was killed in a "yew alley" were some footprints. The last sentence of the chapter, which I read in a scary voice, was "Mr. Holmes, they were the footprints of a gigantic hound!"

I could see Abby walking toward us, for sure coming to tell us that we had tack to clean or stalls to muck out. Da said, "No surprise there."

I said, "Yeah, but what's a yew alley?"

"Probably two lines of yew trees leading away from the house. I've seen some of those. They are huge and old. The trunk looks like it's been woven out of some other tree trunks. That's the spooky part, if you ask me." I made up my mind to go to the library and look yews up. Maybe Ruthie would draw me a picture of one.

I closed the book.

Yes, Abby wanted us to do some work, but it was to help her carry the hose around to the tanks, fill them to the brim, and give the horses some cooler water to drink. The hose is long. There are three different faucets. One of them is on a post at the far end of the gelding pasture. She had put Jack back in his stall – all the hay was eaten – and maybe because it was hot, all the horses, even Gee Whiz, were just standing around, finding whatever shade they could. When we were in the middle of doing this, she said, "Well, listen to this."

I said, "What?"

"My dad's truck broke down in Arizona."

"Are the horses okay?"

"He wasn't hauling the horses. A guy in the hauling business is going to bring them next week. I guess he bought two. Both geldings."

Da and I looked at each other.

"But he's got to wait a few days to see if they can fix the truck."

I did not say what my mom would say, which is, "Can he afford to fix the truck?" because my mom is always worried about what things cost. I said, "He should trade it in. My dad could get him a good deal."

"He was going to trade it in last spring, but then decided that he likes it too much, and didn't. It isn't that old – only about five years. I guess he ran over something in the dark that broke an axle. Anyway, I hope he doesn't decide that he loves Arizona so much that we have to move there."

And I hoped that she was kidding.

And what popped out of my mouth was, "Can I spend the night?"

Abby said, "You should. You can stay tonight and tomorrow night."

"Can I sleep in the barn?"

Abby laughed. She said, "You can sleep in my room. I have a trundle bed that you pull out from underneath mine. Da is in Danny's room."

"How's Danny?"

"He's okay. He's up in Oregon, near this town called Ashland. He told Mom that he's shoeing horses again, but who knows. I guess there are lots of forests up there, so maybe he's hiking all the time. I think he's written Mom twice since he got back."

I knew where he had got back from – Vietnam. But that was all I knew. Da and I helped her coil the hose and then she carried it back to the barn and set it off to one side, by the barn faucet. I went into the house. Abby's mom was sweeping the kitchen floor, and after I walked in, she swept right behind me. I said, "Abby said I could spend the night, tonight and tomorrow night."

She said, "That'll be fun."

"Do you mean that?"

She smiled and patted me on the head, then said, "Yes, but only if you like corn on the cob."

"I love corn on the cob."

"Well, there you go."

I looked at my watch, then said, "I'd better call Mom."

Mom hadn't left to pick me up yet, because Joan Ariel was still napping. She said, "That's fine. Do you need me to bring you some clean clothes?"

I thought of Da, who seems to wear the same thing every day. I said, "No. Let's see how dirty I can get."

Abby's mom was behind me. She said, "I can loan you a nightgown. Abby has some things she's outgrown."

So there I was, on a sudden horse vacation. I was very happy.

I looked at my watch. Before I got the chance to spend the night, the day had seemed as though it was coming to an end. Now it stretched ahead of me like a long road. At least three hours until dinner, and then more reading, I thought, and then lying in the dark near Abby, with the windows open, listening to the horses, and maybe sneaking out of bed and looking for them in the moonlight.

Right then, because the back door was still open, Rusty, their dog, came trotting in with something droopy in her mouth, looking very proud of herself. She laid it gently on the floor at the feet of Abby's mom. I'd never seen anything like it – it had really long legs and long ears and a black tail. Abby's mom said, "Wow."

Rusty sat down and gazed at it.

I said, "Is that a rabbit?"

Abby's mom said, "It's a hare. A jackrabbit."

"How did she catch that?"

"I don't think she knows. Open the door as wide as you can." The hare's ears were flicking. I didn't see any blood on the hare or on Rusty's mouth. Abby's mom said, "I think she surprised it. She's fast and she's quiet."

The hare moved again.

I sneaked around it and pushed the door against the wall.

Abby's mom looked at Rusty and said, "Rusty, stay!" Then she took the broom and very gently eased the hare toward the door and out onto the back porch. By the time she got it through the door, it was turning its head back and forth. She said, "Close the door."

I did, and we watched it through the window. Rusty watched, too. The hare rolled around for a bit, then seemed to come to, as if it had fainted. Then it sat up, the way Easter bunnies sit on their haunches, and flicked its ears again. Then it seemed to look around and say, "What just happened?" It jumped down the steps. Rusty had her paws on the windowsill and she gave one bark, and then the hare was gone – around the house to the left, fast as lightning. I saw that my horse vacation was going to be very interesting.

I said, "Why didn't she kill it?"

"Well, for sure she's not hungry. But it's more like she hunts for sport. A few months ago, I was over in the hay barn and she was with me. A bird had been looking for oats, and it flew out. She leapt into the air and caught it without even thinking about it. It was just a natural movement."

"Did you let the bird go?"

"Of course, but it didn't survive."

"What kind of bird was it?"

"A sparrow."

She went into the closet and got a mop, then mopped the spot where the jackrabbit had been, and I went out the front door to look at the lemon tree and smell the blossoms.

When I came back in, Abby was lying on the sofa. She said, "Mom is going to the market. You want anything?"

"Gravensteins."

"She'll look for those. I am going to take a nap."

"I'll be quiet."

"Don't get into trouble."

"I'll read a book. I'll read *Charlotte's Web*."

She nodded and her eyes closed.

I found the book and went out to the back porch. No sign of the hare. I decided to read the part where the spider, Charlotte, starts writing words in her web. I wished she would write "deduction," but I don't think Charlotte ever read any Sherlock stories.

From Abby's back porch, I could see part of the mare pasture and part of the gelding pasture, the front of the barn, and the strip of land between the two pastures. Everything was still. I read a chapter, then I heard a little noise, so I kept quiet and stopped reading. I thought maybe the hare had come back, had decided that I could be its friend. I'd heard of people having pet bunnies, and even walking them on a leash. I could go into the house, if I was quiet enough, and get a carrot. I set the book down. There was another sound, and then Da eased out of the barn, just like he was sneaking somewhere. He was carrying a lead rope and a halter, and he had his hard hat on. I opened my mouth and then closed it. He was also carrying an apple, which I hoped was not a Gravenstein. It took a long time, but he did walk all the way to the end of the gelding pasture, where he climbed over the fence. I stood up so I could see better. Ned was a little way up the hill, picking out leaves or something. Da looked at him, and a moment later, Ned picked up his head and looked at Da, then trotted toward him, halted. Da held out his hand, giving him the apple. He put the halter on Ned, which was not a problem, because Ned dropped his head and was quiet. Then he led Ned to the fence, climbed to the top rail, and slipped onto Ned's back. I watched for about ten minutes, then I stepped quietly off the porch and headed to the far end of the arena.

I might have noticed Da, but it didn't seem like he noticed me. He was sitting bareback on Ned the way he always sits on a horse – as if he were glued there. His legs hung down, and his back was straight but flexible. He was holding the lead rope with his right hand and petting Ned with his left, first at the base of his neck and then just behind where he was sitting. When I got closer, I heard that he was humming, and the song he was humming was "Waltzing Matilda." His humming was slow and soothing. Ned walked here and there. I would have expected him to try and put his head down and graze or to look around, but he just walked here and there. Da would shift his weight a little from side to side, or push one leg against Ned's ribs, and Ned would turn. Finally, when I was about four steps from the fence, he saw me. Ned pricked his ears, and Da made a funny face and said, "You caught me."

"Just tell me one thing, because I understand everything else."

"What?"

"Why did he come over to you?"

Da whistled four sharp notes, kind of high, a little like a bird. Ned glanced around at him and pricked his ears, then Da slid off, landed on his feet, threw the lead rope across Ned's back, and trotted away toward the middle of the pasture. I stood next to Ned. Now Da whistled those birdie notes again, and Ned trotted over to him. Da handed him something from his pocket that was small like a lump of sugar.

I ran over to them. I said, "He comes when you whistle? Like a dog?"

Ned said, "I am not a dog."

Da said, "All of our horses do, so I taught Ned. They each have their own whistle." Now he turned toward the other geldings, and made another whistle – one that went high, then low, then high, then low – and here came LB, trotting straight to Da. I thought when he got to him, he would sit like a dog and prick his ears, waiting for his next command. But he paused, then went to Da and sniffed his pockets. Da showed him his hands, open wide. No treats.

I said, "That's too bad!"

"Well, you have to not give them something once in

a while, or they get bored. They want it more if they only get it sometimes."

He led Ned to the fence again, this time putting the lead rope to the other side, and threw himself onto Ned's back. Why was I impressed with this? Abby rode him all the time. But always fully tacked, never bareback, never just wandering around as if they didn't have a thing in the world to do. I said, "How often do you ride him?"

"This is the eighth day in a row."

"How do you keep it secret? Or did Abby say you could do it?"

"She didn't, but I also didn't ask permission. I do it when Abby and her mom are busy. I bet if her dad was here, he would have caught me. We don't do much. Some days it's maybe twenty minutes, some days no more than ten. The other morning, I told Abby I would get up and do the morning feeding, and I got up a half an hour early and rode him when the sun was rising."

In my own mind, I said, "Why didn't you tell me about this, Ned?"

Ned said, "You never asked."

CHAPTER 11

I knew what I had to do. I petted Ned on the nose, then went back into the house. I tiptoed through the kitchen into the living room. Abby was still sleeping. I wasn't going to be the one to spill the beans, as my grandma would say. I took the Sherlock book and went out onto the back porch. Da came, and I started reading again.

The next part is Sherlock and the visitor talking about what the visitor saw. I tried to do Sherlock's voice a little low and the visitor's voice a little high. It turned out that the yews were not trees, but hedges "twelve feet high and impenetrable." Da said, "Oh, I've seen that in England. The gardeners trim them so they look like stone walls made of leaves."

So the yews made a long tunnel, and there was a gate at each end. The part I loved was where the visitor could tell how long Baskerville stood near the *wicket-gate* by how many ashes his cigar dropped. I liked that word, "wicket-gate," but didn't get as far as I'd wished to. Da was sitting up and paying attention – every so often he would nod his head. In a scary voice, I read the line "Several people had seen a creature upon the moor which corresponds with this Baskerville demon, and which could not possibly be any animal known to science. They all agreed that it was a huge creature, luminous, ghastly, and spectral." Da and I were paying such close attention that we both jumped when Abby, who was suddenly standing behind us, yawned and said, "How much have you read?"

Da's mouth opened in a silent scream and he fell backward. Yes, he made me laugh.

I said, "Not very," and showed her the page.

She said, "Oh, I read a couple of the stories, but I haven't read that yet."

I said, "I'll leave it for you and take *Charlotte's Web* home."

Abby kissed me on the top of the head.

Da sat up.

Abby said, "Time to hand out the hay," yawned again, and we went down the steps.

I said, "Did your mom tell you about the hare?"

"No. What hare?"

So as we were walking to the hay barn, I described what Rusty did, no exaggeration, since it was interesting enough all by itself. Then I said, "Is Rusty a hound?"

"As far as we can tell, Rusty must be half German shepherd and maybe half Australian shepherd. She would get the quickness from the Australian side."

Da said, "Can she sing 'Waltzing Matilda'?"

Abby said, "If any dog could, she would be the one. We never figured out where she came from. We don't even know how old she is. Mom sort of took her in. Dad looked around for lost-dog posters and called the pound, but no reports. A few years ago, when she first came to live with us, she caught a young bobcat. Maybe that was a sign that she started out with a family, but then lived on her own for a while."

Rusty is a friendly dog, and I've petted her about a million times, at least when she's around the house, which isn't often, because she spends a lot of time up the hill and down by the river, *investigating*, but now she looked to me a little like a *giant hound,* and I wondered where she had come from after all, and if she had ever seen a *yew alley.*

We put the hay into the wheelbarrow and Abby pushed it. On the way out, Da and I carried the hay flakes to the gelding fence. I would hold them while Da climbed over, and then I would give them to him through the fence and he would carry them here and there. I watched Ned. Ned watched Da. Once in a while he pawed, but he didn't follow Da the way the other geldings did. Ned was the last to get his hay. It was a nice pile and he ate it all by himself. Da gave him a few pats before he returned to the fence. On the way back, we fed the mares the same way. After Abby put the wheelbarrow where it belonged, she checked the water troughs. Since we'd filled them earlier, we only had to carry a few buckets to top them up. We got back to the house. I was panting like a dog, since we'd been talking so much about dogs, so Abby filled a bowl with water and showed it to me, then set it on the floor. I got down on my hands and knees and was about to try lapping it up when Abby's mom came in the door with some bags. I wanted to get Da to laugh.

For dinner we had lasagne, something my mom

likes to make, and boiled beets, which Da was willing to eat, and fresh string beans given to her by someone from their church who she'd run into in town (they were good). It was still light, so I went out for a walk while Abby did the dishes and Da did the drying and Abby's mom picked up her knitting. I wanted to have a little talk with Ned.

As I walked around, I could smell lots of things, the way you can in the evening, but I couldn't tell what they were – maybe what I smelled was a mix of everything. The sky was clear and dark blue. Since the mountains are to the west of the ranch, the sun was about to go behind them, but not exactly down. It was sitting just above the ridge, and the shadows of the fences on the golden grass were dark and exact. The trees cast shadows, too, long ones that stretched away from the trunks. I knew that Abby would go out just before bedtime and check on the horses, to make sure that no one was, say, stuck under a fence or colicking. Between you and me, this is the bad side of having your own place – you have to watch out all the time for something that might have gone wrong. Even if you only have your own horse and not your own place, you have to make yourself not think about what might go wrong all the time or you would never get your homework done, much less go to sleep. As far as I could see, nothing had gone wrong since we fed, and I picked up my step to walk away from my bad thoughts.

Ned was standing quietly, slightly up the hill, at the far end of the pasture. He heard me coming, looked at me, and nickered. I had no carrots, and I held out my hands, open and empty, but that was okay. I tried the whistle: four high notes. His ears flicked and he came to the fence, and I went to him. I climbed onto the first rail and reached across to pet him on the side of his face and down the neck. I hoped that was enough of a reward for coming to the whistle. He was smooth, as if he'd had a bath, but I knew he hadn't. Some horses, like Ned, seem to rub off the dirt, to go from gritty to silky in a couple of hours. Others, like Gee Whiz (I looked up the hill), look dirty all the time. Abby's dad once told me that greys know they can be seen from far away, and get dirty in order to hide themselves, but I don't know if that's true. Gee Whiz does like a muddy spot better than anything, and in the winter, if there is one, he will find it and roll back and forth like he's never been this happy before.

Ned stood quietly. His eyelids lowered a bit, as if he

was enjoying the petting. I said in my own mind, "Are you always good with Da?"

Ned said, "Yup."

I said, "Why?"

"Because he's always good with me."

"What does that mean?"

"He doesn't kick me or use the whip or snatch my mouth. He doesn't use a saddle."

"Abby is good to you!" In my own mind, I sounded a little shrill.

Ned didn't answer. Instead, he backed away, turned, and went looking for some bits on the ground. I climbed over the fence. I went over to him and started petting him on the shoulder and then along his side and back. I walked around behind him, staying close and gently dragging my hand along, because you always have to be careful, but mostly they kick you if they're surprised, and if you're right next to them, they can't really kick you. But Ned didn't try. I started petting the left, first his face, then his neck, then his side. He lifted his head and took a few deep breaths. I said, in my own mind, "Tell me."

"I see something and jump, and that bit grabs me

in the mouth and it hurts, and then she pulls me back even harder."

"She wants you to stop running off."

"It hurts. I can't help myself."

"What's she supposed to do?"

In my own mind, Ned said, "I don't know. But I feel it in my mouth all the time, and it makes me jumpy."

"Horses don't understand cause and effect."

Ned said, "Who told you that?"

"Everyone."

Ned said, "Everyone is wrong."

I thought to myself, "Of course they are," then said, "Do you like Da better than Abby?"

"I like the way he rides me."

It was now getting actually dark, so I finished petting Ned and walked through the pasture toward the house. I decided not to think about what he said, because the pasture was dry and bumpy, and I didn't want to stumble and fall down. Then when I got to the house, Abby's mom opened the door and said, "I was about to send Rusty to find you."

I said, "If I'm lost, chances are I'm where Ned is."

She smiled.

Then, because they don't have a TV, we sat around the coffee table in the living room and played a game called whist, which I had to learn, but I liked, and Da said it was the same as bridge, but more fun. I had to learn to shuffle the cards when it was my turn, and at first they would just fly away, but I figured out how to hold them after a few minutes. I went with Abby and Da to check the horses, and everything was fine – a relief – and when we were walking back, I told Da that Abby's window would be open, so I would be sure to hear him if he went out onto the roof, and I would tattle, and by the way he smiled before he said he would be good, I knew he had at least thought about going out onto the roof, even if he hadn't done it. And I had got my laugh, sort of.

Abby and I went to her room, where she handed me an old nightgown and we pulled my bed out from under hers. The only place to put it was right below the window, which was fine with me, because her window looks toward the pastures, and all I would have to do to see the horses in the middle of the night would be to get up on my knees and peek out.

Once we were in our beds and the lights were off, I let myself think about what Ned had said.

And the first thing that came into my mind was Ruthie, the sad look on her face the last time I'd seen her. I'd tried to investigate and find out what was wrong, but no witness with a "stick" was there to tell me anything, and no gossip trail like the one back where we used to live led to any information, because Mom didn't know anyone well enough to gossip with yet (though maybe she would get there with the neighbours who were the parents of Joan Ariel's new friends). But maybe, I thought, the look on Ruthie's face wasn't sadness because something had happened; maybe it was fear that something was going to happen. A lot of bad things had happened to Ruthie and her mom – her dad had stolen some money from the place where he worked and run away. Then they lived on nothing, and Ruthie was so thin that not only was she not eating, she didn't really want to eat, unless it was a peanut butter and strawberry jam sandwich or a cookie that Melanie Trevor or I might give her. She was small then, smaller than I was, and she always looked at her feet (though, until I pointed it out, she never noticed that her socks needed pulling up). Now she is taller, though still thin. When we moved here, and there she was, a surprise to me, she looked as though everything was new and different. And then she turned out to be the one of all of us who could draw anything she wanted to. But lying in bed, I thought that maybe she was like Ned in the gelding pasture – there had been so many bad things that she couldn't get them out of her mind for long. Something she might hear her mom say, or a postcard she might find lying around – *anything* could make her afraid that all the good things were going to go away again. Her house, her mom's bookkeeping job – even all her pencils and paper, for heaven's sake – might just disappear. Then I thought about buying her some extra pencils and paper and leaving them around somewhere where she could find them, though at the moment, I couldn't think where.

Abby was sound asleep. She was lying on her side with her back to me and the blanket pulled up to her ear. She wasn't snoring. I got up on my knees and looked out the window. Da was not on the roof, though for the moment, I wished he were. I looked at my watch. It was 11:34. I also wished I could see the horses, but I couldn't – the clouds had come in, so no moon. I could hear them moving around, and I could hear branches creaking, and I could hear the house creak, too, which houses do in the night. An owl flew out of one of the nearby trees – right out of it, I guess because that's where its nest was, inside the tree. First it hooted, and then I saw the wings spread, and then I saw it fly over the top of the barn, quietly, and disappear into the darkness. Maybe I was the one who should go out onto the roof, just to see what I could see. I've heard of people who stay up most of the night and sleep most of the day, and while I was staring out the window, I could understand why. The night is very interesting. It occurred to me that maybe Ruthie loved to draw because it helped her stop thinking of what might happen and got her to think of what was happening right now.

And then, sometime, I must have fallen asleep, because I woke up later on my back in the bed, no covers. I woke up long enough, that is, to notice that I was uncomfortable, and straighten out and pull up the blanket. Then I went back to sleep and slept all the way until it was bright daylight and Abby came into the room from giving the horses their morning hay. She said one word, "Pancakes," and I sat right up. She said another two words, "Maple syrup," and I was out of bed. She said, "You don't have to get dressed. That nightgown is like a full-length coat on you."

Da was already at the table. Abby's mom gave him a plate with a stack of pancakes – five of them, all crispy edges. I did yawn, but it seemed as though I had gone straight from my dream about walking around our old town, up and down hills, looking for the car because my dad had forgotten where he'd parked it, to sticking my fork into five perfect pancakes. I said to Da, "Did you have any dreams?"

"I dreamt that Tater was in my room, sitting on a chair in the corner."

"Was he playing whist?"

"No, he was reading a book."

I said, "He would if he could."

I wasn't sure that Da had really dreamt this, but I liked the idea so much that I didn't ask. It was a much better dream than mine. Was Da my best friend? It seemed like every day we got along perfectly, tossing words back and forth and catching them. But if he was my best friend, then it would be very sad to see him leave after knowing him just a month, and our friend-ship would have to end the day he walked out the door.

CHAPTER 12

It was going to get hot, so Abby said it was time to ride. We put on our riding clothes and went out the back door. The night before, things had been peaceful, but now the geldings were arguing over every pile of hay, and Gee Whiz was trotting here and there, snatching bits from all of them. I've always liked Gee Whiz, because he's so beautiful and talented and gives Abby a great ride, but now I thought he was a bully, and didn't like him at all. I jumped over the fence with the lead rope and ran to Tater, who was minding his own business. I took Tater out, over to the grooming area in the barn. Abby was there, straightening things up. I did not tattle on Gee Whiz. Anyone can see it. I curried and brushed Tater, got my saddle and bridle, just doing all the regular stuff, and then, right when I unsnapped Tater from the cross-ties to put on his bridle, there went Da, and he was riding Ned, bareback, halter and lead rope. Three steps past the doorway of the barn. I put Tater's bridle on, without buckling the throatlatch, and led him through the door. Da and Ned were walking into the arena. Abby called out, "Ready?" Then she said, "Go on over. I have to put Jack in the round corral." She sounded totally normal. I guessed that she hadn't seen a thing.

Mum's the word, as my grandma would say.

I buckled the throatlatch, then led Tater to the mounting block and got on without taking my eye off Da and Ned. They did just what they had been doing in the pasture, wandering here and there. Ned, with his head dropped, seemed very relaxed. Gee Whiz whinnied, and Ned looked up the hill, but he kept walking. I went through the gate and closed it, started walking Tater, and here they came. Tater did not put his ears back, Ned did not put his ears back. They walked (we walked) along together. Because Tater was going straight down along the railing, Ned did, too. When we got to the far end, Da looked at me, I looked at him, and we smiled. This would not be a secret much longer, but it felt like the biggest secret ever.

Da said, "Trot."

I did what I was told. Tater did what I told him. And Ned trotted along beside us. Da sat quietly, even at the trot, like he was glued to Ned's shiny back. We turned at the next corner, kept trotting, and there was Abby, with her hands on her hips. I glanced at Da. He nodded one time and pushed Ned a little in front of us. Tater and I followed, trotting nicely, until Da sat deep and came to a halt. He smiled, the way the boys who know how to get away with things always do when they are caught. And I smiled just because I thought that.

Abby said, "What are you doing?"

Da said, "Watch." And he rode Ned here and there, all around the arena at the walk and the trot. It wasn't much, and they didn't jump, but Ned looked calmer than I had ever seen him. Even when Gee Whiz whinnied and he and Beebop ran down the hill, bucking and kicking, all Ned did was glance in their direction and keep on trotting.

Abby never stays mad for long, and she didn't this

time, either. She said, "That's interesting. He looks totally relaxed."

I said, "Da has a theory that results from his investigation."

Abby chuckled. "What is it?"

I said, "I'll let him tell you," and pushed Tater up into the trot. We went after Da, but even when we came up behind Ned, he just kept trotting along. Abby kept watching us, and I can't say that we did much – not like a regular lesson – but finally, after we'd been walking for a few minutes, Da went over to Abby and sat deep. Ned halted.

Abby said, "I'm impressed."

Da said, "He's smooth as silk, isn't he?"

"You should try his canter."

Da said, "I have." And he backed Ned, turned him, lifted into the canter, went in a larger circle, and came back. Abby's mouth was open, and so was mine.

I said, "I thought he was just walking."

Abby exclaimed, "You never told me?"

But I didn't have a chance to say anything, because Da brought Ned to a halt, slipped off, and looked at me. He said, "Get on him. I'll give you a leg up," and in spite of the fact that I was scared to death, I jumped off Tater, handed the reins to Abby, and stepped over to Ned. I bent my knee, and Da hoisted me onto him, which was a good hoist, and maybe more than Da expected, since he grunted. Now I was sitting there, holding the lead rope, and Ned walked away. Here's what it was like:

I could feel his back and his sides, moving forward, shifting left right left right, just a little bit.

I could feel my own body settle in and relax along with his.

The lead rope seemed like enough – I held it in my right hand and put my left hand on his mane. I scratched him a little bit.

When he lifted his head up, I could feel his back get firmer. When he dropped it, I could feel his back get softer.

I could feel in my own body where each one of his legs was and where it was going.

A bird flew out of a tree. Ned tossed his head, and I could feel that from the top of my head all the way down to my feet, but then I gripped the lead rope a little more tightly and loosened it, and he dropped his head again.

I sat deep and he halted and sighed.

It was not like riding a horse and doing well. It was something else. And I didn't have to talk to Ned, even in my own mind. I already knew what he was thinking. He was thinking, "How are you? I'm fine. What's over there? Oh, just a bird. I like that breeze. It's cool. Where's Tater? Oh, he's okay. What is Gee Whiz doing? Oh, same old same old. Sigh. Turn right. Go straight. Turn left. Circle back to the others." As we walked toward him, I saw Da chattering to Abby, and Abby, I have to say, was paying close attention to what he was saying.

I felt very brave. Just to try it, I pressed my legs against his side and said, "Trot." He picked up a trot, and it was like no trot I've ever ridden – smooth and easy and moving along. I shifted to one side, and Ned turned. I put myself back in the middle and Ned went straight ahead. I thought, "Sit deep," and he halted. He blew out some air. We were facing away from Da and Abby, and for a second, I thought that I had no idea how to get back to them, but then I turned my body and laid the lead rope across Ned's mane, and he turned, too. We walked back to Abby and Da, easy as you please.

I slid off Ned and then handed Abby the lead rope. Here's a thing that I've noticed over the years ("Ha," my grandma would say, "not many years, you're only eleven"): some grown-ups get upset just because you are being disobedient. What it seems like to me is that because they've told you not to do something, you're in trouble because you did it. A perfect example of this is something that happened in the spring. It was afternoon recess, and I saw one of the boys – Arturo – bounce a golf ball off the wall of the school and catch it. Mr. Oakley walked over to him, stood by him, and then held out his hand for the ball. He was behind Arturo, so Arturo didn't see him, and he threw the golf ball against the wall again. It bounced back, hit a crack in the pavement, and I guess because it was a golf ball and not a tennis ball, it flew up and broke one of the school windows. Mr. Oakley grabbed Arturo by the arm. Arturo was staring at the ball, and he was startled, so he bumped against Mr. Oakley and knocked him down. About six of the boys started laughing at Mr. Oakley, and I was the one who said, "Why did you grab him? He didn't see you!"

Yes, my voice was loud. Ruthie put her hand over her mouth.

Mr. Oakley got to his feet, pointed to the golf ball, and snapped, "Pick that up, young man."

The boy next to Arturo, Dougie, bent down and picked it up, handed it to Arturo. Then Mr. Oakley said, "Douglas! Did I tell you to pick that up?"

Dougie is pretty shy, and it looked like he shrank into himself. Well, I couldn't help myself; I said, "He was being nice! You should be nice!" And then all three of us got sent inside to the principal's office, and I got a note to take home that said I'd been "insubordinate." When she read the note, Mom laughed and said, "Nothing new there," but then she sat me down and we talked about tact and asking questions instead of telling people what to do.

But Abby isn't like Mr. Oakley. She just got on Ned and said to Da, "Show me what you've been doing," and they walked around the pasture, talking. I got on Tater and followed them. Da walked along beside Abby and Ned, and he would talk, but he would also move, to demonstrate how he was using his body to get Ned to do things. Ned stayed quiet until Gee Whiz screamed out a whinny, and then he pinned his ears and tossed his head, but he didn't run off. I did see Abby tense up.

I said, "Gee Whiz is mean and Ned is afraid of him." Abby asked Ned to halt, then looked around.

I said, "He told me that. He wants to be with Sissy. All the geldings are like a gang, and they bully him."

Abby didn't tell me I was crazy. She said, "I've seen that, but you don't put geldings in with mares. My dad wouldn't allow that."

And then I said, "Well, your dad won't be around for a few days. You could try it." And Ned tossed his head, just like he was saying yes.

Since it was really weird to think that Abby was having a lesson that Da was giving her, I decided to tell myself that what we were all doing – Abby, Da, Ned, me, and even Tater – was gossiping. And then it was fun. Abby did try a little canter on Ned (he was good in both directions), and I cantered on Tater, three big figure eights with only two trot steps for the lead change. Then it was so hot that Da went over to one of the trees and lay down under it, and Abby and I took Ned and Tater to the water tank before we untacked them. After that, I took Da a glass of water that Abby's mom came out on the porch and gave me. Da sat up and drank it all the way down – not exactly gulping, but more like pouring it in. I said, "Do you think I was crazy to say that Ned is talking to me?"

Da said, "No. One thing is, you can think whatever you want. The other thing is that horses do communicate all the time. Maybe what seems like talking to you is just you seeing how they're behaving and understanding it in your own way. You talk all the time, so that's your way."

I said, "I do talk all the time, even when I don't know that I'm talking."

"You think I haven't noticed that?"

And then we both laughed.

I saw Abby do it. I saw Abby lead Ned over to the mare pasture and open the gate, and Ned walked right in. Sissy came over to say hi. She didn't pin her ears or threaten him; she just wandered around, nosing for this and that, and after a few minutes, Ned started to follow her – at a distance, because Ned is always careful, but as if he was her friend. Abby watched them for a while, and then for the rest of the afternoon, one or the other of us would go check on them. He seemed to fit in. He didn't boss them, and they didn't boss him. Abby said that that was because Sissy is the boss mare, and if she accepts someone, the others do, too. When we were walking back to the house for dinner, I said, "Are you being insubordinate?"

Abby said, "I think I'm being independent."

That is a good word, much better than "sassy," "disobedient," "contrary," or "willful." There is, after all, the Declaration of Independence. We learned about it in fifth grade, and there isn't a Declaration of Sass. I decided I was going to be independent for the rest of my life.

For dinner, we had baked potatoes and petrale sole, which is a fish that they catch out in the bay where we used to live, so of course that started me talking about whales and boats and dolphins and sardines and herring, and then I realized that everyone else was being very quiet, so I shut up and ate my fish, which was very good. After dinner, Abby and I went out to check on Ned and the mares again, and Ned said, "Why bother? Everything is fine. I like Sissy, and she likes me." We walked around in the twilight and listened to the birds. Abby said that she was going to buy a book that would help her be a bird-watcher, and I said that maybe Colonel Dudgeon would give her bird lessons, not riding lessons.

She said, "I would pay for that."

When we came back, Abby's mom had finished the dishes, and everything was quiet, so quiet that I thought it was rather spooky. Abby's mom had been knitting on the couch in the living room, but she was dozing off – her hands were in her lap and her head was on the back of the couch. We tiptoed through the room. The spookiest thing was Da, in the kitchen, sitting at the table, reading *The Hound of the Baskervilles* all by himself. He didn't seem to notice us, so I kept tiptoeing, and touched him on the back of his neck, very lightly. He jumped and made a noise. I sat down at the table.

He pushed the book toward me.

I said, "Were you reading without me?"

"No. I was looking at the parts we already read." He pointed to the next part, and the first interesting words that I read aloud to him were "Waterloo Station." This part was about someone who now owned the yew alley and the house and everything, was "coming to claim it." Sherlock piped up and said, "In your opinion there is a diabolical agency which makes Dartmoor an unsafe abode for a Baskerville." I said to Da, "Would you like me to translate?" And then I did: "You think the devil makes Dartmoor a dangerous place for a Baskerville to live." But I did like those words, "diabolical," "agency," and "abode." I kept reading, and Da paid attention the whole time. We went to check on Ned again. No diabolical agency or unsafe abode. Sissy and another mare were lying down, Ned was finishing his hay, and the breeze, at last, was cool.

CHAPTER 13

I had a good night's sleep and got up with Abby to give out the morning hay. Everything in the mare pasture was still fine, and I could see no evidence of kicks or bites on Ned. We passed out the hay, as always, to the geldings first, and then to the mares. I carried the hay across the pasture while Abby watched. The mares went to their piles. No one tried to shoo Ned away from his pile. In the meantime, over in the gelding pasture, Gee Whiz and Beebop were having an argument – lots of squealing and whinnying and running around over what looked like a regular old pile of hay. At least Gee Whiz knew enough to stay away from Beebop's hind end. Ned looked up the hill one time, and I am sure he said, "Good riddance," but maybe that was me talking.

When we went back to the house for breakfast, I was ready (and imagining blueberry muffins or popovers, or something else delicious), and then when we came into the kitchen, there were a woman and a man I had never seen before – the woman looked like Da, so I knew she was Da's mother, and the man looked like a leprechaun. He was so short and spry, as my grandmother would say, that I expected him to jump onto the table and do a dance. But it was true that when he opened his mouth to introduce himself to Abby, he had the Colonel Dudgeon voice. Boom boom, all around the kitchen, "Nice to meet you, young lady! I've heard about you!"

Da's mom came up to me and said, "You must be Ellen. Jane told me about you." She was nice – she was the kind of woman who takes your hand in one of hers and pats it with the other. She had a big smile that made her whole face light up. Da looked really happy to see her, and I could completely understand why Jane would be friends with her. She was also about a half a head taller than Colonel Dudgeon. I decided that it was her job to ride the big horses and his to ride the small ones. We sat down for breakfast, and yes, there was a treat, something I've never had before called pigs' ears, which didn't have a thing to do with pigs. They were crispy, crunchy cookies shaped a little like hearts and about as yummy as any cookie I ever ate.

Abby's mom gave us scrambled eggs and bacon and peaches and Gravensteins, plus some toast. Colonel Dudgeon ate like a horse; Da's mom ate like a bird – that is, she pecked at this and pecked at that, including a pig's ear, but no bacon. Colonel Dudgeon never stopped moving or talking – you could see why he needed the feed. But when Abby asked what horses they had found, he zipped his lip, and Da said, "He never tells."

After breakfast, we got dressed and went out for our lesson – me on Tater, Da on LB, Abby on Gee Whiz. Of course I wanted to do a good job – I felt sort of like I was at a horse show and Colonel Dudgeon was the judge. Once we were in the ring, Da's mom called out the commands – sometimes to all of us, and sometimes to one of us – and Colonel Dudgeon stood in the middle. Well, maybe he thought he was standing, but really, he was walking around and hopping here and there. I was sure that he'd had a miserable time in school because there are those boys (mostly boys) who look like their desk seats are on fire and they can't sit still for more than a second or two. If I were the teacher, I would let them do all their work walking around the room, but no one has asked my advice, at least not yet.

Tater was his usual good self, did everything as soon as I asked, and once I had watched Da pushing LB to lengthen his stride, I tried the same with Tater, and of course Tater was very agreeable, and stepped under and moved forward. I did loops and serpentines, and cantered when I was told to, and trotted and halted. The colonel watched Da the least, me the second most, and Abby on Gee Whiz the most. He would stare at Gee Whiz for a long time, then look at me. It was like his eyes were binoculars, wide open. When it came to the jumping, Da's mom told Da the course: not too high, but complicated, or intricate, as my mom might say. He jumped it while I watched, and then I jumped the same course. We came down to the walk and left the ring. Colonel Dudgeon raised the fences to four feet, and Gee Whiz began his round – eight jumps, three loops, his ears pricked, his mane and tail flying. Didn't touch a thing.

When Abby came down to the halt and dismounted, Colonel Dudgeon was on Gee Whiz in a minute. He leapt on like he had springs, and he rode the same course, and then two other jumps, an oxer and a coop with poles across the top. I'm guessing that the coop jump was four feet six inches, maybe four feet nine. And Gee Whiz was almost but not quite himself. He went fast, but he was a little more limber and paid a little more attention to the colonel than he had to Abby. But maybe that was because the colonel was curled on top of him like a jockey, his arms stretched forward and his head up, like he was staring right between Gee Whiz's ears. He came down to the trot and then the halt and jumped off. He said, "Decent fella." But I could tell by the glint in his eye that he meant more than that.

I said, "How high is that coop jump?"

Da's mom said, "Four feet nine inches."

I said, "That's high."

She smiled one of those grown-up smiles that means, "Well, okay, if you say so."

Da had dismounted, too. He said, "Tell her the story."

His mom smiled. I could see that "don't encourage her" look in her eye. I said, "I guess I can't dismount until I hear the story."

So she clucked, but she said, "Oh, my. Well, when I lived in Australia as a girl, they had a kind of class where you choose your own course, and all the fences are a different height."

I said, "I saw one of those at the show. It was called Gambler's Choice."

She went on, "Yes. The more you jump, the more points you get, and you get the most points for the highest ones. So, my horse was about fifteen hands, small, but not a pony. Lovely jumper, though. I trotted into the arena, and he was just feeling so perky that I turned and went over the biggest one, then the second biggest, and so on. My trainer was furious, because he had told me to go slow and try out the smaller ones, but we did win."

Da said, "Tell her how big the biggest one was."

"Well, it was a wall. It was five feet six, as I remember."

I said, "Taller than your horse! How could he see over it?"

"He couldn't until he leapt. He was willing, and also very sure-footed."

And I did gasp. So did Abby. I heard her.

Abby was now back on Gee Whiz, and then she and

Da and I rode out across the hillside. The horses had had plenty of work, so they walked along on a loose rein. I watched Da's mom and Colonel Dudgeon wander around. They stopped and looked at every horse, front, side, back, other side. I could see that they just couldn't help themselves. I could also see another thing – our car, Mom at the wheel, pulling in through the gate and stopping by the house. I realized that my horse vacation was over.

Mom seemed to be in a hurry. She said that the pot roast was in the oven, so that meant we had to get home before – and then I forgot what time we had to get home before. I did untack Tater, wash him down, and put him in his pasture, where, because he was totally wet, he rolled back and forth in the dirt and got himself completely dirty again. Da was somewhere, and Abby was hurrying to tack up Mordecai, so she waved good-bye, and that was that. It took me half the trip home to remember what day it was – Saturday. And Mom and Dad had got a babysitter, because they wanted to go to a music concert at the fairgrounds, and so it was rush rush rush, and then, boom, our early supper was eaten, they were gone, Alice, the babysitter, was yawning in front of the TV, Joan Ariel had gone to bed early, and it was still daylight, so I decided to take a walk and let all the things I had learned over the past two days wander around in my mind until I could figure out what I felt about them. I shouted to Alice, "Taking a walk!" and closed the door before she could say anything. Then I went once around our little park and over toward the school, and maybe because I wanted to think about things, the next thing that happened was, I ran into Ruthie, and I mean that I ran smack into her, because I was looking down the street and she was backing up, and bump, there we were. She turned around, and good for Ruthie, she had the world's biggest grin on her face. We were across from the park, so I said, "Let's go over in the shade," and she followed me.

In some ways, all I needed to know was that she was smiling and happy and here. But of course I said, "What's going on?" and she told me that a man who owns an art gallery in the town near ours where all the galleries are (my grandmother took me there once, when she was looking for extra-special Christmas presents) had told her he was going to hang two of her sketches – one of a condor and an oak tree and one of three blue jays and a rosebush. He wasn't going to tell anyone how old the artist was, and he didn't promise that they would sell, but he wanted to see what customers might think, and he had a lot of customers. Ruthie put her hands on my shoulders, stared at me for a moment, and said, "I don't know what to think!"

I said, "Think about making another picture."

She said, "First, I'm going to think about jumping up and down," and she did – ten jumps down the sidewalk along the park until she sort of collapsed on the grass under one of the trees and lay there with her hands behind her head, looking at the sky through the branches and smiling.

I went over and sat down next to her. I said, "Are you a genius?"

But I shouldn't have asked that, because her face went blank and she looked sad again, so I said, "I didn't mean that." And then I was honest with Ruthie. I said, "I only meant that I don't know anyone like you, and that is the most interesting thing about you. You do everything your way."

Ruthie said, "That's you! That was how I got the idea to do what I wanted, keeping my eye on you.

Remember when you got caught holding the lid of your desk up and looking at something, and then Miss Cranfield startled you and you let go of the lid and banged your head?"

I said, "Kind of."

"Well, I couldn't stop wondering what you were looking at, so one time after that, when everyone was going out to recess, I stayed back and looked in your desk. I saw your drawings. In fact, I leafed through them and decided that you were as bored with school as I was, and that drawing was a good way to pass the time."

"You never drew before that?"

"Off and on. But I would leave my pencils around and lose them and forget where the paper was, so I stopped. But then, when you were reminding me about pulling up my socks and buttoning my sweater, I decided always to put the pencils in the same place, on the windowsill by my bed, and then I started drawing every day, and my aunt liked it, so she bought me more pencils and more paper."

I said, "And the more you did it, the more you liked it."

Ruthie sat up and laughed. "The more I did it, the

more I had to do it. I didn't like it every day, but some-times when I didn't like it, I wanted to do it even more."

One thing that is really strange is spending a lot of time watching someone, and not realizing that they might be watching you, too.

Ruthie said, "Once you start looking at things and drawing them, then there are more things that you look at and want to draw. I drew this bird that was perched on a branch outside my window. I had to do it fast, because after a few minutes, it flew away. I looked at my picture, and realized that I didn't know what kind of bird it was, so I showed it to Mom and she said, 'Well, maybe a woodpecker or a flicker,' so then I talked her into buying me a book with pictures of birds, and there were so many!"

I said, "Colonel Dudgeon knows all about birds."

"Who's that?"

"This leprechaun at Abby's place."

"A leprechaun has moved into Abby's place?" She looked confused.

I said, "You come with me Wednesday and you can see him for yourself."

We got up and went around the park, pretending to be horses – walk, trot, canter, jump – and it was fun.

I'd never talked with Ruthie that much before, and it seemed totally normal.

Pretty soon, the sun was sitting on the trees to the west, and I knew I had to go home. I didn't know whether to tell Ruthie to go home, too, so I looked at my watch and said, "Uh-oh."

She said, "What?"

"It's eight o'clock."

"Do you have to go home?"

I nodded. So I did go home, and Ruthie did, too. And when I got there, Alice was still watching TV and didn't seem to know that I'd been gone. Just to be sure, I peeked into Joan Ariel's room. She was waking up, but she wasn't crying. I went back downstairs and walked over to Alice and said, "Boo!"

Yes, she jumped.

CHAPTER 14

On Sunday, right after we got back from dinner at Grandma and Grandpa's, the phone rang, and it was Abby. Since Abby never calls on Sunday, I got scared, but the first thing she said when I answered the phone was that Tater was fine.

I said, "How about Ned?"

"He is, too. Sissy's taking good care of him. Can you come for your lesson tomorrow?"

"I don't see why not."

I asked Mom, who said yes, and then Dad said he would drive me because he had a one-year-old used Cadillac to test-drive. Cadillacs are very fancy, and I'd never been in one, so I thought that would be fun. I spent the rest of the evening sitting up in bed, reading a book I found in the bookcase, *The Trumpeter of Kra-kow*. I didn't understand a thing in the book, including what "Krakow" meant or what was going on, but I read it anyway because after every page, I would figure something out. So it was like *The Hound of the Basker-villes*, except that I was the detective, not Sherlock.

In the middle of the night, I woke up and wondered how I would tell Ruthie that I was going on Monday rather than Wednesday, but then I "resolved that difficulty," as Sherlock might say, by deciding to insist that I would also go on Wednesday.

The Cadillac was parked on the street in front of our house. It was bright red, about a hundred feet long, everything edged in silver, and a convertible. Mom doesn't like convertibles. Dad says that's because she doesn't want to mess up her hair, but Mom says it's because of things flying through the air, and when she says this, I imagine a flock of birds swarming around the top of the convertible like a big, sparkly black cloud. When I was putting on my riding clothes, Mom stopped by the door to my room with Joan Ariel in her arms, and said, "Don't forget to fasten your seat belt," and then she sighed. By the time I'd got the carrots from the refrigerator, Dad had put the top down and was grinning. Just by looking at him, I knew he didn't care about his hairdo, but he also didn't wear a hat, because that might fly away, too.

The red Cadillac zipped along, smooth and fast. Dad made a couple of detours, just to check how it took corners, but I didn't mind. I liked the things I saw, the sunshine, the things I smelled. I figured Dad would drive it all over the place before taking it back to the dealer. I said, "Is a Cadillac a Ford?"

"No, it's General Motors, but we can sell any brand of used cars."

"What did the owner trade it in for?"

"A red Mustang."

I entirely agreed with the owner, except I would have traded it in for a chestnut mustang.

The thing was, Dad didn't leave as soon as I got out of the car (hoisted myself over the side). He got out, too, and here was the colonel. They shook hands, and walked away over toward the pasture, but they didn't get all the way there – they walked back and forth, talking, and while I was watching them, Da ran up to me and said, in his Colonel Dudgeon voice, "Sell me that pony!"

I said, "You! Why would you want Tater?"

Da said, "I don't, but the colonel does. He's got some girl up in somewhere who needs a safe pony, and they're willing to pay."

And that was the very moment when I realized that I did love Tater, maybe without even knowing it.

Da said, "Your mouth is hanging open."

Well, maybe. I closed it, but I knew exactly what I was going to do. I stared at Dad and Colonel Dudgeon, and just like I was calling them, they walked toward me, Dad with his hands in his pockets and a serious look on his face, and Colonel Dudgeon hopping here and there, smiling.

I didn't say anything, and neither did Da. He was standing behind me, so I imagined him doing back-flips. Dad said, "Well, Ellen, something has happened, and of course you should be the first to know. The colonel, here, has a client who wants to buy Tater. I don't know what you think. . . ."

I said, "Only if I get to buy Ned."

The colonel's face popped in my direction, and I could see right there something Grandma would say: "Why in the world?"

I said, "I love Ned."

The colonel's head shook a little. I could read that, too: "Silly girl." And yes, Abby's dad had owned Ned for a long time and had never been able to sell him. But I'm not a silly girl. I know what I want and I know why.

Dad took the easy way out. He said, "Well, we'll see." Then he looked at his watch and told the colonel that he had to get to work, so they walked over to the Cadillac and talked another minute while Dad was getting in, and then Dad drove off. I watched him. You could see that Cadillac from miles away.

The colonel didn't say anything to me, but he did pat me on the shoulder and walk toward the house. I said to Da, "When do you have to go home?"

Da said, "They say tomorrow or the next day. It's a lot cooler here, or at least, down by the ocean, where they're staying, so I think they're putting it off a little."

"Why aren't you staying there with them?"

"I like it better here, and Abby's mom doesn't mind. I guess the dad is getting home late tonight."

"He'll make you behave."

Da said, "We'll see." So there were a lot of things we were going to see.

Abby came out of the barn, and we walked over to her. Tater, Mordecai, and Gee Whiz were already in the barn. Tater was in the cross-ties, and he did nicker, very softly, when he saw me. I kept the carrot in my pocket, went over, and petted him down the side of his face and along his neck. His ears were relaxed, so I knew he was enjoying it. I did wonder what he would think of a new place. "Up north" for Da isn't very far up north – less than a hundred miles, Da says – but maybe I would never see Tater again. I brushed him all over with the soft brush, admiring his red-and-white coat, how it changes from the front to the back and the top to the bottom. The good ponies keep moving because we outgrow them, so maybe Tater was a world traveller, as much as Gee Whiz. But of course, Tater would never tell Gee Whiz off, and so Gee Whiz would never know.

Then, as we were riding, I heard Da say to Abby, "Did he offer you a good price?"

Abby nodded.

"What's your dad going to say?"

Abby said, "Take a guess."

Da said, "My guess is he's going to ask for more."

Abby said, "They'll work something out."

I trotted a little to catch up with her and said, "Are you talking about Gee Whiz?"

Abby said, "Yup," and went up into a canter and looped around the far end of the arena.

Da said, "The colonel thinks he could be an event horse. I'm sure he's got a buyer in mind. Gee Whiz would jump everything, because good Thoroughbreds do, but Abby's also got him moving very nicely, so he could do the dressage, too." Then he said, "And he's big enough for a man, so that helps."

I was thinking of the look on Abby's face, and I said, "Did you ever have a pony that you didn't want to sell?"

"Yes. I didn't want to sell Hollister. I had him when I was seven. He was a palomino. I had a tantrum when Mom sold him, and she didn't say a thing, she just let me have the tantrum, and then she put me on a pony she'd bought, named Ridgemark, who was a little bigger, and Ridgemark was so comfortable that I enjoyed him instantly. And then, when I got off and was leading him into the barn, Mom said, 'If we hadn't sold Hollister, you wouldn't have Ridgemark, so you think about that.' That was the only thing she said about my tantrum, so I learned not to have tantrums anymore."

"But didn't you miss him?"

"I learned not to. I like trying them all out. They're all different. Look at the kids at your school. They're all different, right?"

I thought of Ruthie, and of Jimmy Murphy. I said, "Yes."

"Well, horses are like that, and don't let Colonel Dudgeon tell you they aren't. They notice different things, they like different things, and they understand things differently, but the main thing is that they feel different. As soon as you get on, you know that pony or that horse is just himself, and that's the best part."

I thought, "No, the best part would be getting to know one really really well." Like Ned, for instance. I thought of something my grandma says: "Well, you can't have it both ways." I wondered if that was true.

Now Abby came trotting back and we had our lesson, nothing new, just enjoying ourselves, practising the patterns and movements that we'd been working on. We didn't jump, and I knew why without Abby telling me – if you're about to sell your horse, then you have to be careful that he doesn't hurt himself, even a little bit. Then, when we were riding along the hillside, in order to keep myself from staring at Ned the *whole time*, I asked Da what event horses had to jump. He said, "In the last part, it's just like a horse show, but the part I like the best is the cross-country. There are all kinds of jumps made of logs and brush. You have to gallop through water and jump onto banks and then off of them. There are chairs and coops. They aren't terribly high. It's fun."

I said, "I saw those types of jumps outside the show arena at the stables."

"They do eventing there."

"Do you gallop into the woods?"

"Of course."

I took a deep breath, thinking about the piney fragrance. I said, "Gee Whiz can jump high."

Da said, "He loves to gallop. I think he would like eventing more." And, I kid you not, just then Gee Whiz shook his head (he was about twenty feet in front of us) and let out a loud whinny.

I was thinking about what Da had described — galloping and jumping and galloping, over the hills and through the woods. I said, "What do you think, Ned?"

And Ned said, "We'll see."

We caught up to Abby. She still wasn't saying much, but I saw her look down the hill at Jack So Far, and I could read the look on her face — now that Gee Whiz would be leaving, she could think about Jack more, decide what was next for him, start riding him. And he was her darling, no two ways about that, as Grandma would say, because she'd known him since the day he was born. And maybe, if the other horses got trained and sold (including the ones her dad bought in Oklahoma), then she might never have to sell him.

I did a good job untacking Tater and cleaning him up and giving him a few bits of carrot. All three of us – Abby, Da, and me—were pretty quiet. I knew that not only would Tater soon be gone, but Da would, too. I let that thought circle around in my mind. I knew I would miss him, but I also knew that things would calm down, and maybe, just maybe, I would be a little relieved. Then I was going to read some more of *The Hound of the Baskervilles* to him, but just when I opened my mouth to suggest it, there came the red Cadillac. I asked Abby if, when I came back Wednesday, I could bring Ruthie, and she said, "Well, of course. She should draw a picture of Gee Whiz."

"Is that a commission?"

"Let's say it is."

"I'll tell her he's grey. Is Colonel Dudgeon going to be here?"

"All day, I'm sure."

"Ruthie can talk to him about birds."

"They can take a walk. He likes to do that. He says that because the ocean and the mountains and the fields and the trees are so close together, there are lots of types of birds around here."

Wednesday was going to be a big day.

CHAPTER 15

Of course Ruthie knows where my house is, but because I've never seen her here, I was shocked, dumbfounded, taken aback, floored . . . all those words, which I love. Let's say I was a little surprised when I was walking down the stairs and looked through the window in the door, and there was the top of Ruthie's head. I opened the door. She turned around, smiling. She had a bag, full, I was sure, of pencils and paper. I said, "Abby wants you to draw a picture of Gee Whiz."

"He's gorgeous."

"Do you have grey pencils?"

"All pencils are grey. He'll be like a black-and-white photograph on a golden background with a few green trees."

"You've looked at him before."

"When I was there, he was whinnying all the time."

I said, "You want some breakfast?" She shook her head but followed me to the kitchen, and when Mom set a piece of bacon and a poppy-seed muffin in front of her, she ate them right down.

Mom took us to the barn. Dad was already gone, and along with him – "Thank goodness," Mom said – the red Cadillac. Mom did not drop us off. She parked, got out, and followed us to the barn, but the colonel and Da's mom weren't there yet.

I could see Da opening the gate to the gelding pasture, then leading LB out. Tater was standing behind LB, flicking his ears and waving his tail. Then I saw him glance at me and toss his head. But his ears stayed pricked and he didn't run up the hill. I trotted toward him, and he actually nickered again. When Da saw me, he said, "The dad is back."

I said, "Did he make you clean six stalls before breakfast?"

"No, but we straightened up the feed room. He told me that his motto is—"

I said, "Do it now."

"That's what he told me."

I walked on to the gate, and Tater put his nose through the railings. I tickled him a little bit between the nostrils, then took his halter off the hook and opened the gate. He looked like he'd spent the night rolling in dirt. Even his cheeks were grimy. But I didn't mind brushing him. Because of the summer weather, his coat was smooth – I would use the soft brush, which Tater seemed to appreciate. I decided it was like petting, and my first thought was that I should brush Ned to see if he liked it, and my second thought was that horses don't get petted much, sometimes on the face or just in front of the saddle. At horse shows, you see riders have a good jumping round and because they're happy, they give the horse a couple of smacks on the neck, and I know they think they're praising the horse, but why wouldn't the horse see this as a slap?

I looped the rope over a railing outside of the barn, did the brushing, and combed Tater's mane, too – and here came Colonel Dudgeon, hopping and skipping toward us, already laughing. "My girl!" he said. "Haven't you done a lovely job!" Just then, Abby's mom came over with Mom and introduced her to the colonel, and I went into the tack room to get my saddle and bridle. I did turn my head and look at them. They talked and talked. I waited. And then the colonel put his hand on Tater, and I knew they'd made a deal.

I put my saddle back on the rack and trotted out of the barn toward them. The main thing I did just then was look around for Abby's dad – there he was, up the hill, with his hand on a fence post. I saw him jiggle it. So he'd been gone for almost three weeks, and everything had fallen apart, and he had to *fix it now*. I knew my job was to find things out, and right then I thought of a way. Ruthie was next to the round corral, where she was looking at Beebop, and why he was in the round corral I don't know – no one dares to ride Beebop. Beebop is a friendly horse, though, and he was kind of leaning toward Ruthie, inviting her to pet him. She looked cautious. I went over to her, showed her how to pet Beebop a little bit on his shoulder, then I said, "Let's go look for Abby and see if she can put Gee Whiz somewhere where you can see him."

Ruthie followed me. We found Abby in the feed room. Did she look sad? I couldn't tell. I said, "Ruthie's here. She's ready to draw a picture of Gee Whiz."

"Oh, okay." Yes, she was sad. So the colonel had made an offer and her dad had accepted it, that was my *deduction*. She walked away and Ruthie followed her. I dawdled, and then I got my wish. Da came over, carrying LB's bridle, and said, "Five thousand dollars."

I spun around. "For which one?"

"Gee Whiz. Abby's dad looked like he'd been hit over the head with a hammer. But a good hammer. They're taking Gee Whiz to the East Coast. Horses are way more expensive there. I'm sure he'll get a lot more for him."

"How much are they giving us for Tater?"

"Fifteen hundred."

I grabbed his elbow. I said, "How do you know all of this?"

"You think I can't hear Colonel Dudgeon? His voice is like a church bell."

"Doesn't your mom try to hush him up?"

"No, she just laughs."

"Where is she? I don't see her."

"She stayed in town to have her hair cut."

I knew what I had to do. I waited for Da to leave – I was sure he had something planned – and when he did, I went out of the feed room and walked straight to the mare pasture. I had three carrot pieces in my pocket. Ned and Sissy were standing under a tree, nose to tail, with their heads down, switching their tails back and forth a little because of flies. This is how horses cooperate when there are lots of flies. Very lightly, I imitated Da's high Ned whistle, and Ned lifted his head. I showed him the biggest carrot piece, and he sighed, then idled in my direction. Yes, it was now hot. That was good. I looked at all the halters hanging on the railing, picked out Ned's. When he got to me, I slipped between the rails, gave Ned his bit of carrot, and put on the halter. I walked him around a little bit, asking him to step over, and then I petted him on both sides. He wasn't as dirty as Tater had been, but he was pretty dirty. Then I led him to the fence, climbed to the top rail, and got on. I didn't look left or right. I didn't try to see if anyone was coming. All I did was keep petting Ned under his mane.

One good thing about Ned is that his back is smooth and easy to sit on. Some horses, like Gee Whiz, have big withers and prominent spines – I don't see how you could ride them bareback, but there I was, thinking all these thoughts, and then Ned began to walk around. He wasn't trying to eat grass, and he wasn't stopping or going fast; he was just walking, and in my mind, he said, "Where to?" I said, "Along the rail," and turned him slightly. I didn't kick him or push him hard with my legs. He went along the rail. It was like he was going for a walk and didn't mind taking me with him. Sissy watched us for a minute, and then she came, too, a few steps behind us. The other mares, who were a little further down the hill toward the dry creek, didn't seem to notice.

And I thought, this is what I really like – not going to shows or taking lessons, but just being with them, feeling them under me and near me. I put my hand behind, on Ned's back. It was warm and smooth. And then, it happened – a coyote with pointed ears and a furry tail appeared between some trees a little way down the hill. It looked pretty small, skinny with long legs, maybe young. Ned and Sissy both lifted their ears and one of the mares whinnied. Then another mare whinnied – it was like a signal going around. But all Ned did was look at the coyote and look away, then walk on, and I saw that maybe because all the horses at Abby's ranch live in the pastures instead of in stalls, wild animals were no big deal. I said, "Ned, I think you're more afraid of what a person might do than what an animal might do," and he tossed his head.

Yes. I thought about that time when I slipped onto Ned in the round corral and rode him for maybe a minute. I remembered how excited I'd been, how a minute had seemed like forever, and then Abby had come running out of the house with the news that Jack So Far had won some money in a race. Jack So Far was older now, and so were we all. What was the stranger thing – that I was sitting on Ned, wandering around the pasture like it was no big deal, or that so much time had passed since that moment, and yet I'd never forgotten it?

I admit that I did sort of forget about all the grown-ups, so I was a little surprised when we turned back toward the fence, and they were standing there, Mom next to Abby's dad, Abby's mom next to Colonel Dudgeon, and Da and Abby off to the side. I didn't see Ruthie, but I was sure she was busy with her "commission." I didn't go all the way to the fence. I squeezed my thighs, and Ned halted and flicked his ears. Sissy went over to what was left of the hay and ate a few bits.

I saw Abby's dad's mouth open and I glanced at her mom, who was hiding a smile. My mom looked like she didn't know what in the world was happening. I said, in my Colonel Dudgeon voice, "Mr. Lovitt, I'll give you fifteen hundred dollars for Ned. Take it or leave it." I saw Da nod his head and then stick his tongue out at me.

Abby's dad's mouth closed right down and his eyebrows lifted. They went really high, too, let's say right up to the brim of his cowboy hat, which he then pushed back with his hand.

He cleared his throat and said, "Actually, I think, since I understand that you are selling Tater, that Sissy is a better match for—"

I said, "No thanks. Sissy is a good horse, but the best match for me is Ned."

He said, "Ellen, you make me laugh, but you're ten years old—"

"I'm eleven."

I saw what I needed to do. I pulled a little on the rope, got Ned to turn, continued walking around, and then, when I got to a spot that was a little open, I clapped him with my legs and said, "Trot." He trotted. And yes, I did stay on, and the reason I stayed on was that Ned has maybe the smoothest, easiest trot I have ever felt. It didn't bounce me; it sort of cuddled me. We trotted in a pretty big circle. I squeezed my thighs and he halted. I said, "I know what I want."

And Abby's dad said, "Well, you always do, I'll admit that."

Mom was nodding.

I said, "Ned would like to stay in the mare pasture with Sissy."

Abby's dad said, I kid you not, "That does seem to be working."

And then, two of the geldings I didn't know ran across the gelding pasture, squealing and kicking up. My heart skipped a beat, but Ned just glanced at them. I walked him to the fence and slid off. I held out my hand to Abby's dad, and he came over and shook it.

I petted Ned a few times down the neck and took off his halter. He stood there, quietly. I put my arms around his neck and give him a hug. I wasn't stupid – I knew that he was more mysterious and less reliable than Tater, that not everything was going to be perfect, but that was a good part, the step-by-step part that would be a fascinating puzzle that I would spend years figuring out. I also knew, I really did, that he was my friend, and that I would treat him like a friend. I gave him the rest of the carrot, and he took it very carefully.

Mom and I sat with Colonel Dudgeon on the porch, and Mom told Colonel Dudgeon just to give the money for Tater to Abby's dad. Then Ruthie turned up, and Colonel Dudgeon said, "Well, I hear you're interested in birds!" and Mom said, "Birds are interesting!" So the three of them went on a walk around the ranch. Ruthie left her bag on one of the chairs, and I peeked into it. Yes, there was a drawing of Gee Whiz. I didn't take it out, but I could see that it was so good, you could almost hear it whinny. I decided that Ruthie was my friend, maybe my best friend, now, since there were things that we shared with each other that we didn't share with anyone else. And if you love a horse, you know that a best friend can stay mysterious. I sat by myself for a little while, enjoying the breeze and smelling something sweet, though I didn't know what it was. I thought maybe bushes and plants and trees were interesting, too. There are a lot of things to find out about, that's for sure.

And that's why I forgot, until the last minute, to say good-bye to Da. Mom had the door open, waiting for me to get into the car, and I knew we had to go. I suddenly remembered that Da would be leaving the next day and I knew I wanted to give him a hug or something, but I couldn't see him anywhere, not even on the roof of Abby's house. I looked and looked, but finally all I could do was ask Abby to give him a hug for me, and she said, "I'll give him one for me, too. I'm sure he'll be back."

That night, I couldn't get to sleep. The door to my room was open. I could hear Dad snoring across the hall. Everything else was totally silent, so I knew Mom was sleeping, and Joan Ariel, too. My room was mostly dark, with a little moonlight flickering through the trees, and when I paid attention, I could hear a light breeze, which was why it was flickering. I sat up and closed my eyes. Immediately, I saw Ned next to Sissy, under a tree, down by the dry creek. I said, "Where's the coyote?"

Ned looked around, sighed, looked at me. He didn't say anything, even in my own mind. But that was okay. I didn't care whether he was talking to me anymore. The feeling I got from petting him, sitting on him, having him walk and trot underneath me was enough.

Soon, sometime, we would canter, and that would be heaven on earth, as Grandma would say.

And it was fun to spend more time with Ruthie. We walked around the neighbourhood. I did the talking; she did the drawing. Some days, she would point things out to me – say, a bird or a tree – and I would go home and look them up, then tell her what I'd learned the next day. We both liked exploring.

A few weeks later, two days before school started, I got a letter from Da. His handwriting was fine, and he spelled most of the words correctly. He said that he was enjoying his new pony, named Delinquent, that his mom had found in England, a Dartmoor pony, about the same size as Mordecai. And in case I wondered, because of the word "Dartmoor," yes, he had read *The Hound of the Baskervilles* all the way to the end. The letter reminded me of how much fun I'd had with him (as if I would forget) and I wondered when I would see him again. The good sign was that his mom and Jane were best friends. That meant that I could be a pest until Jane invited them back. I do not mind being a pest. When I wrote to Da the next day, I made sure to say that everyone missed him, including Rusty, who kept howling his name, "DAAAAAAAOUUUU." That made me laugh; I hoped it would make him laugh, too. In the meantime, I sneaked that book, *The Pale Horse*, out of the bookcase and took it up to my room. It wasn't exactly scary, though there were some witches, but there wasn't actually a horse. My favourite part was that there was a town named Much Deeping. That is a town I would like to visit.

JANE SMILEY

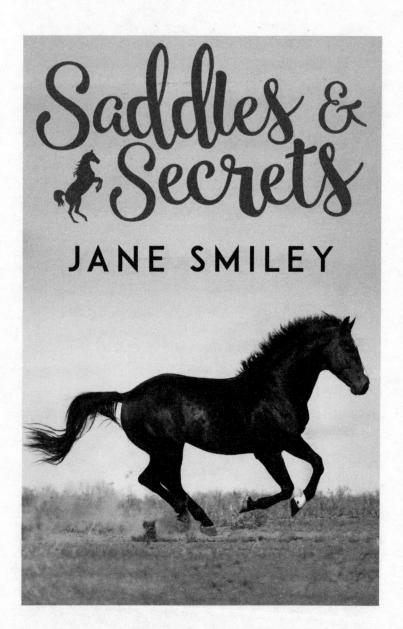

Saddles & Secrets

JANE SMILEY